Jackal in the Dark

David Patrick Beavers was born on January 30th, 1959, in a
tiny California town in coastal Santa Cruz County. While
growing up in a working class environment and
manoeuvering through a public school system plagued by
fluctuating 'guinea pig' educational programmes, he became
aware of the contradictory social and political philosophies
of first half Baby Boomers and the previous generation's.
They were constantly at battle and sending conflicting
signals to him and his peers, members of the second half of a
generation of Boomers and the first members of Generation
X. Upon graduation from high school, he moved to Los
Angeles to attend the University of Southern California
where he earned a BA in Drama. It was during those
undergraduate years that he developed his gay identity, got
sober and focused on an awareness of belonging to a
generation unlike that of his predecessors. Upon completion
of college, he bounded around from city to town pursuing a
career as a playwright and survival job opportunities, finally
landing in New York where he enrolled at New York
University and earned an MFA in scriptwriting. He has
since relocated back to Los Angeles to work as a scriptwriter.
While having done many projects for theatre, television and
film, *Jackal in the Dark* is his first novel.

Jackal in the Dark

David Patrick Beavers

Millivres Books International
Brighton

First published in 1994 by Millivres Books (Publishers)
33 Bristol Gardens, Brighton BN2 5JR, East Sussex, England

Copyright © David Patrick Beavers, 1994
The rights of the author have been asserted

A CIP catalogue record for this book
is available from the British Library

ISBN 1 873741 16 2

Typeset by Hailsham Typesetting Services, 4-5 Wentworth House,
George Street, Hailsham, East Sussex BN27 1AD

Printed and bound by Biddles Ltd, Walnut Tree House,
Woodbridge Park, Guildford, Surrey GU1 1DA

Distributed in the United Kingdom and Western Europe by Turnaround
Distribution Co-Op Ltd, 27 Horsell Road, London N5 1XL

Distributed in the United States of America by InBook, 140 Commerce
Street, East Haven, Connecticut 06512, USA

Distributed in Australia by Stilone Pty Ltd, PO Box 155, Broadway,
NSW 2007, Australia

To Sebastian Beaumont and Peter Burton
for their understanding and acceptance . . .

To Carron V Leon, David Richey, Kiki Hall, Tracey Barone
and Laura Toffler for their consistent support through the
walk of life . . .

To Everyone finding their way along the path . . .

for
RSR

Jackal in the Dark

There's the dark of your place inside me; the dark of the time when you take shape. A visitation. I know your touch, your scent. Over-ripe apples and damp, tilled soil belie the sweat. An honest sweat of an honest man doing an honest day's work. I was born from a jackal's blood clot buried in darkness beneath desert sand. I've a vicious nature. A nature that only softens at night. At your time. I miss you now. I shouldn't have been true to my bloodline.

❋ ❋ ❋ ❋ ❋

It was 1968 in 1978. A time warp peopled with recognizable faces all running rampant through that grand old Victorian house on Menlo Street. People I knew. Some I liked. Some I didn't. A party given to celebrate the glory days of the Haight. A party given for the simple purpose of getting high. An excuse to get high. I'd come with Jill, a domineering young girl with long brown hair and a beach bronzed face. Jill dove straightaway into a bottle of bourbon peppered with mescaline. Her objective was obliteration.

Darren met me with a pyrex pot boiling over with yellow-jackets, black beauties, hearts and crosses. I wanted a sting. Yellow-jackets and beer. I liked beer. Too much, perhaps. I was getting soft in the gut.

To think about it, the party was pretty lame. Most of us had been about a decade old in 1968. A lot of vague recollections. Mostly of television programs. We had no cause, no banners to fly, no roles to perform. The generations of adults in the fifties and sixties left little for us to seek out that hadn't already been explored and exploited. Whatever the passions they had, we lacked. A deficit.

We felt good at times, but not passionate. Jill, Darren, Michael, Erica, Tracy, David, Laurie, et al. Everyone in that grand old house that night had a dark place within them. A place negated by the mind. Unfilled by the soul. A place that had been sealed, brick by brick, until no light ever

1

slipped inside. Just the darkness that readily vomited out when even the smallest brick was tapped.

Jill and I spat our darkness, our blackness, out on each other constantly. We'd seen what we believed to be the worst of each other innumerable times. If words could get bloody, then we flooded her house read. Always her house. I was her 'brother.' She and Sue, Connie and Laurie, shared a house. Sorority girls with their own special sisterhood. I was their adopted brother. We fought. We'd fought about attending this party while under a sea of eyelet lace trimmed down in Sue's big bed. Big decisions, big debates, big battles always took place in Sue's room, in Sue's big bed.

Jill had been dumped. I was her 'brother', remember? Not her lover. Dumped by a man named Dan, whom I never really liked.

She was upset. Dan was to be at the party at the grand old house on Menlo Street. Jill wanted to see him. To get obliterated and vomit her misery down the front of his shirt. I thought that was pointless. She didn't. We argued about the merits of vomiting all over Dan. I conceded. She won. We went.

I wanted a sting. The yellow-jackets Darren had given me made my face flush. Blood pumped ferociously. Beer kept my veins open. Cigarette steam kept them closed. Drink - open. Buzz. Puff - close. Buzz. My head was a hive that night. I left Jill early on in the evening. I refused to think about the misery she wanted to put herself through because that misery would become mine by the end of the night. I wasn't in the mood for that. Jill always won our battles. She had to win. Maybe that's what filled her own dark place.

I sat on a footstool. Jill and Dan were across the room, next to the old, blistered fireplace. The Moody Blues drowned out their words. All words. I heard nothing but the buzzing in my head. Dan spoke. Jill spoke. Dan spoke again. A smug expression on his face. No vomit. She slapped him. She slapped him with a half full glass of bourbon. The glass shattered on Dan's chin. A minor cut.

2

Bourbon down his shirt. Fellow party-goers ignored them and continued to fill their own hollow spots with alcohol placebos. Dan left. Jill smiled and floated over to Clark. I wanted to go home. I felt empty. Very tired. Very empty.

Hands were on me, massaging my neck, shoulders rolling my head from side to side. I could smell apples. Bare feet wrapped in leather loafers. I saw denim covered legs at my sides. I touched the hands that touched me. Rough. Thick. Your hands. You were there. You were not a part of us. Weren't like us. Nevertheless, you were there.

You asked me if I wanted to walk. I didn't know you, but I wanted to do something. I rose. You were behind me. I could sense your height. Your breath brushed my hair. I looked about the room with a dizziness never before experienced. I could see the buzzing now that was inside my head. A populated buzzing - peopled with faces and names and smells.

"Want to dance?"

The words confused me. Jay was there in front of me. His hips swaying. Pelvis thrusting. I could see his erection prominently displayed beneath his jeans. I'd seen his cock, had his cock, many times before. He was great in bed, but not out of it. He didn't want to dance. He wanted to fuck. We were out to perfect sex.

Your hands weren't on me anymore. No more warm breath. The apple scent was gone, replaced by the stale, stale odour of cigarettes and pot. I spun around, panicked. You weren't there. I turned back. Jay's fingers were already down my pants, crawling across my ass.

We fucked in the next room, half on the sofa, half on the floor. There were no doors to close. People moved freely through the room to get to the kitchen. Everyone saw us, but nobody looked. It wasn't interesting. Others, I knew, were fucking elsewhere in the house. Fucking each other to try to keep from feeling dead. I could hear Jill. I knew her moan. Soft. Low. Animal. She must be with Clark, I thought, as Jay's cock slid in and out of me. He came inside me, then turned me around to suck my uninterested penis. I watched him, but felt nothing. I could see others, near us, gyrating,

3

panting and sweating with their own pleasures. Anyone else would call us depraved, degenerates with our thumbs stuck out for a ride to Hell. But we knew that wasn't true. We were all wanting the same thing - to fill our dark places, if even only for a night. Michael moved from Laurie, his dick still wet with her fluids, and proceeded to fuck Jay. I slowly disengaged myself from Jay's mouth and dressed.

I wanted to shower, but there was only an old claw tub in that old house. I filled it a third full with scalding water and bathed. I washed Jay away. I washed the party away. Soap felt good.

I dressed again, lit a cigarette and went outside. I was alone. The black shadows of the avocado trees and their fallen fruits seemed to float in limbo. I was at the bottom of the sea.

"You want to walk?"

Your voice was soothing. A wave of sincerity lapping at solitude. You looked blue as you emerged from the moon drenched shadows.

"Yeah," I said. "I do want to walk."

Your arm closed about me, drawing me into you. Again, the smell of apples. A hint of sweat. Your body was warm, your shoulder gentle as we walked down the driveway, past a row of vacant cars, out into the street. All the houses on Menlo were dark.

"What do you think about?" you asked.

I pulled away and turned to see you eye to eye. "You're blue," I said.

"Night light distorts," you said.

"Who do you know?" I asked.

You turned and walked back up the driveway. I watched you retreat, hoping to find some recognizable trait in your gait. You walked tall. You walked humbly. I wanted to hate you at that moment. I felt you'd no right to both pride and humility. You disappeared into the black void of the backyard.

I was cold. The fog began to wet me as I stood in the middle of the street staring at the house. Laurie, Darren and Sue stumbled out of the front door. Their cackling cracked the glazed air. They climbed into Sue's old Falcon and sped off. Sue drove well in her blackouts. I'd ridden with her many times before. They only had a couple of blocks to drive. I wanted to go, but couldn't. I lived too far to walk at night.

Headlights cut the blackness. Tires squealed. A horn blared. I jumped between two parked cars. A beer can flew past my head along with the screams of "Faggot!!!" "White fuckin' shit!!!" I could hear the car's occupants laughing the rest of the way down the street. They were from either the Hoover Street gang or La Raza. Two warring clans, one black, one Hispanic, that fought for this strip of Los Angeles.

When their car was out of sight I went back and sat on the porch. I wanted to think. I had to think. I didn't like being alone. I didn't want to go back inside, though. I wanted you to come back to me. Come for the third time. I waited and thought of nothing. When you didn't come, I began to think that you didn't exist. Everything was empty. My own dark place.

I watched as the first tinge of morning sun streaked the purple sky, calling an end to it all. I glanced at my watch. 5:37 a.m. My lungs ached from smoking. I lit another cigarette and drank from the garden hose. A few bleary eyed merry makers staggered out the front door, nodded or waved to me as they passed, then fell into their cold cars.

Two more cars left the line up in the driveway. I could see the overgrowth of weeds beneath the avocado trees. A pick-up was there. The colour was ugly - that of instant coffee with too much cream. I didn't recognize the small truck. I walked up to it and peered into the cab. No one. Then I heard you again.

"Come lay down."

I found you, wrapped up like a burrito in your down sleeping bag in the bed of your pick-up. A greasy lock of hair stuck to your forehead. Brown hair. Pale brown. Fine. Soft. Blue sweatshirt over white. It had a hood. The sleeping bag was green. Forest green. Your eyes. Also green. Your cheeks were as red as Christmas. I didn't speak but climbed into your bed in the bed of the truck. Until I

5

felt your warmth, I hadn't realized how cold I had been.

"You're red," I said.

"Blue before."

"We're watching ten years pass as the sun comes up," I said.

You turned your face to me. You smiled. I felt the first tap of the ballpeen against my internal masonry. Your lips were chapped. I wanted to salve them. You unzipped your sweatshirt and placed my hands inside, between the cloth.

"Thermal underwear," you said.

I smiled. I think I smiled. I don't know. I rested my head beside your chest. You were warm.

"If we wait long enough, the sun will turn this ol' pick-up to gold," you said. I couldn't wait. I fell asleep.

✳ ✳ ✳ ✳ ✳

I awoke at eleven o'clock. Maybe it was one. My vision tends to blur upon awakening. It sometimes remains blurred for hours. I was in my bed, in my room, in my house on 32nd Street. I could hear my roommate talking on the phone in the adjoining room. There was a rap on my door. My roommate, Kurt, stuck his head through the doorway.

"Jill's on the phone," he said.

I groaned and sat up. "Tell her I'll call her back."

"She just wants to know what happened."

"Jay fucked me then sucked me then sent me to bed."

Kurt smiled, closed my door, then relayed my message to Jill. I could hear him through the wall. It wasn't until I stared at myself in the bathroom mirror that I realized that I was wearing your sweatshirt. It was a size too big. My face looked like Silly Putty. My mouth was a barn floor. I hung your sweatshirt on the hook behind the door, threw my own clothes in a heap, then showered. Soap felt good.

Hair combed, face scrubbed and mowed, I put your sweatshirt back on. Again the smell of apples. Sweat. Your sweat. Your smell gave me an erection. Clothes in hand, I crossed the hall back to my room. You must have brought me home, I thought. But you couldn't have. You and I were

6

strangers. Still, I had your sweatshirt on me. I masturbated over your smell. My imagination strove to out-do itself in fantasy. Upon orgasm, it hit me. I might never see you again. My bricks, my dark place - secure again.

Kurt's friends were over for the afternoon. They relished board games - Monopoly, Clue, Chinese checkers. . . whatever. They played every Saturday afternoon. I preferred not to play. Every game ended up in an argument. I could argue with Jill.

I avoided Jill's calls. Kurt finally tired of answering the phone so he unplugged it. He and his friends invited me out to grab a burger at Tommy's. I had a research paper to write. I said, "Thanks anyway." They left. I was alone with paper, pens and at least three dozen books on the development of Harlequin. I forgot about you for a time. I read the books, decoded the pertinent information and classified it all in order to salvage a fifteen to twenty-five page paper that I cared nothing about.

I was in the middle of cutting and pasting notes when I heard the horn. The honking persisted. I left my room and went down the stairs of our old duplex. Jill and Sue were in Sue's Falcon in front of the house nursing Bloody Mary's. Jill held out a third tumbler. I knew that I had to go sit with them. And listen.

"Like the cups?" Sue asked. Darth Vadar's face glared out on the front of the tumbler. "Got'em free with a burger and fries."

We didn't go anywhere. We sat in the Falcon and killed a thermos load of vodka and V-8 juice. Sue rambled. About anything. Jill stared straight through the windshield, sipped her drink and said absolutely not one word. When the booze was gone and there was nothing left to do, I asked Jill why she'd come.

"Jay," she said.

"Jay?"

"Jay wasn't the one in the truck with you last night," she said. "Who was he?"

"Just some guy."

She swung open the car door. "Get out," she said. Sue

7

looked at Jill then back at me. She didn't get it.

"Move your seat up," I said. She didn't. I tried to ease through the narrow space between her seat and the opened door. That's the problem with two door sedans. They inhibit escape. I slammed her seat forward and climbed out. She slugged me in my spleen.

"Fuck head!" she said as she slammed her door shut. I heard the engine start and the car pull away as I walked blindly back into the house.

I worked on the draft of my paper the rest of the day. Kurt and his friends came and went, came and went. Sue called around nine. She'd learned that Jill had seen you at the party. She wanted you. I wasn't supposed to have what she wanted. She knew you wanted me. She had told you that I was supposed to leave with her and Clark, but you told her no. Jill doesn't accept no. Never did. She and Clark quarrelled in front of that old house on Menlo Street. Clark saw you in the cab of the truck as you pulled out of the driveway to take me home. Clark told Jill.

As I readied myself for bed, I stood naked before the full length mirror. I turned to see my back. Jill's fist print was now an aching blue brown splotch. I wrapped myself in your sweatshirt and crawled into bed. I vaguely remember hearing the doorbell. Kurt, ever glued to late night movies, must have let you in. I wasn't surprised to see you standing next to my bed at a little past midnight. A cotton jacket now hiding the same white sweatshirt.

I felt cold again. The bed felt cold. You sat on the edge of my bed, slipped out of your shoes and slide under the blankets with me. I was naked under your blue sweatshirt. I unzipped it, as you had done for me, and opened myself to you. You turned to face me, your denim legs brushing then hugging my own. One arm slid over my ribs, between me and your fleece. The other arm went up. You swept back the bangs from my eyes and smiled. Your hand found Jill's fist print. You tapped another brick in me.

"Nothing's infinitely empty," you said.

"We don't know where black holes end," I said.

"They end at the beginning."

8

Your hands explored my body. Your hands. Rough. Gentle. Thick. I wanted to get up, to prove to myself that you weren't a spectre created by a wet dream. But, she'd seen you. Clark saw you. You were real. There last night. Here in my bed.

"Who are you?"

"Rex."

"Rex?" I laughed a bit. Too unreal. Fictional. You didn't laugh, though. I couldn't tell whether you were hurt or pissed. You had no expression. "I'm sorry," I said. You turned your head away from me. I said it again with a sincerity alien to my mouth.

"Go to sleep," you said. I did.

I woke up at 4:07 a.m. Not 4:10 or 4:15, but at 4:07.

You were sleeping peacefully. Lips parted slightly, semi-fetal, facing me. I wanted to feel your flesh but didn't. I slept again.

The alarm woke me at seven. You were gone. Again gone.

* * * * *

Days passed. Weeks passed. My concentration was slipping. When Jill learned from Clark who learned from Jay with whom I spoke daily that I hadn't seen you in weeks, she started telephoning me again. No mention of our fight, but I knew that she felt a minor victory. I was to come to her house when I'd finished work one night. I was a waiter. A typical job for a college kid.

I showered before going. I didn't want to go, but felt obliged to. I arrived at her house with two six-packs of Moosehead beer. She hated Moosehead. I loved it. A perfect slap.

She said nothing about the beer as we went up to Sue's room. Sue and her Great Dane, Maul - a beautiful Harlequin with one brown eye and one blue - were lounging on the big bed, buried under a tattered old comforter, sipping Diet Pepsi and eating Nestle Crunch bars. A Brady Bunch rerun blared on the vidiot box.

"Hi," Sue said.

9

"Hi."

Jill flopped on the bed. I sat next to Maul. She enjoyed playing shake the rag with my arm. We drank beer, smoked cigarettes, ate chocolate and watched television for two and a half hours. Maul finally tired of us and went downstairs to sleep. I was bored. Sue's yawns signaled that she wanted to sleep - to kick us out of her room and die until morning.

"I've an eighter," she said.

"So do I," said Jill. "We're in the same class, dummy."

"Jill," Sue said, "I want to go to sleep."

Jill threw her a look. "Then go sleep in my bed."

Sue, angrier than a pissed on cat, snatched her pillow and leapt off the bed. Jill settled into the now vacated warm spot. We watched television in silence for another half hour. I got up.

"Gotta go," I said.

"Fine. Pussy out," she said.

I sighed my most obnoxious sigh, dumped the beer bottles, cigarette butts and candy wrappers into a paper bag and crumpled it closed.

"How come we always pollute Sue's room?" I asked.

"My room's too small, stupid."

"Good night," I said.

Jill stared vacuously at the television screen. No "good night", "bye", "see ya" - nada. I closed Sue's door as I left, then went down the hall to the stairs. I met Sue coming up. She had a bottle of Pepto-Bismol in hand.

"I can make you feel better," I said.

Sue gave me a curious, wry look. I indicated for her to follow me into Jill's room. I removed Sue's pillow from Jill's bed and placed it in her arms.

"What's up her ass tonight?" I asked.

"What isn't," Sue said. She leaned against the wall, clutching her pillow. "What's in the bag?"

I smiled and turned back the covers on Jill's bed. I dumped our trash on the mattress. Sue was horrified at first, then laughed.

"You're dead," she said.

"I don't have to live with her."

"She wanted that guy," she said. "That guy in the pick-up truck."

"It's time for me to tell her no," I said.

The door swung open. Jill stood in the doorway. She looked as if I'd gutted her. She wouldn't cry, though. Jill *never* cried. We wanted to strangle each other.

Jill went to her bed and calmly pulled the sheets and blankets up, tossing the ends to the middle, then picked up the bundle and swung it with a vengeance at me. I felt the beer bottles hit. She swung again. Sue tried to intervene. She got clocked in the process. I grabbed the bundle and yanked it away. Bottles skidded across the floor. Jill slapped me. Hard. I laughed.

"Think it's funny?!" she screamed. I laughed again. She slapped me again. We squared off. "Get out," she said.

As I went down the stairs a Moosehead projectile flew over my head. It crashed on the floor. Connie and Laurie, puffy eyed from disrupted dreams, came out of their rooms to investigate. They saw me, the green shattered glass, and Jill at the top of the stairs.

"Assholes," Connie muttered as she disappeared back into her room. Laurie found a broom and dustpan from somewhere while Jill and I continued our stare down. She finally spoke two words - "Forget him." They sounded like a plea to me. Forget him. How could I forget? He - You - were gone. Forever, as far as I knew.

"You have an eight o'clock class," I said. "Go to bed." I left the house and drove home.

I remained awake that night trying to understand that fight. No purpose. No reason. Sheer lunacy by any normal standards. Her words lingered. "Forget him." Forget what I was afraid to feel those two nights you were with me? Just go to sleep, I thought. Sleep, asshole. Drudgery awaits. Breakfast shift at 7:30 in the morning. Oceanography and Biology 110 in the afternoon.

*****

Months passed. More parties. More papers. Spent tips

11

and wages. Jay and I were fucking at least three times a week. I saw less and less of Jill. New men in her life. You out of mine. Spring was coming. Easter vacation.

✻ ✻ ✻ ✻ ✻

I was running with new people. Film students. Mostly Kurt's friends. Jeff, Sam, Dina, Jackie, Lance, Cindy, et al. We went to clubs - Odessy, Studio One - bars like Mother Lode and Blue Parrot. I was filling the dark place inside me with new faces, old dialogue, vodka and tricks. And bath house memberships - The Club, YMAC and the 8709. In the interim, I attended classes, kept a good G.P.A. and continued to work at the restaurant. So what?

While out on the Odessy's dance floor with Jay and Dina one night, I saw you dancing. You were with a young man I knew well. He'd been my lover some years back. I wanted to kiss you. To kill him. Push him in a burning oven and baste him with kerosene. Jay shoved poppers up my nose. You were obliterated in a flash of electric blue.

I ran into him on the patio. Him. Michael. My dark haired, doe-eyed ex. He looked superb. Hair combed, eyes clear and wearing the latest from Fiorucci's. He saw me staring at him. He flashed his capped teeth smile and slid over to me. He said hi, I said hi. We made small talk. He of UCLA and I of USC. Yak yak. Clothes. Mutual friends. Blah-blah-blah. I felt blah. Michael. He had you. Why shouldn't he have you, I thought. He's gorgeous, monied, going places. Michael and I had never fought. We never had much to say to each other. We were beyond being opposites.

"You know Rex?" I asked.

"Who?"

"I saw you dancing in there. To the Village People."

"His name's Rex?" he asked. "Why not. There's got to be one somewhere."

"You don't know him?"

"No. I asked him to dance. We did. He left."

"Where is he now?" I asked.

Michael looked at me. "Are you all right?"

12

I nodded.

"You . . . you want another drink?"

"No," I said. "Thanks, though."

Michael's adept at reading people. A trait I'd long admired in him.

"You here with the old gang?" he asked. I shook my head. He ushered me inside the club, over to a small corner table. We sat. He lit a cigarette. "What is it?"

"What," I said.

"You. You haven't barbed me yet." I'd forgotten about the barbs. My vicious mouth. Fear makes some folks shy. I got caustic. Acidic. Downright mean.

"No point," I said. "Are you happy, Michael?"

"Happy?" He took a long drag off his cigarette. "I guess so. I don't feel like being miserable."

"Smart."

"And you?"

I laughed. Loudly. I felt like a madman for making such a noise. My head fell into my hands. My fingers ran back through my hair. I pulled my head up. "Maybe I enjoy being miserable."

"You enjoy drugs," he said. He hated that about me.

"And sex," I added. He loved that about me.

"Yeah . . ."

I looked into his eyes. Doe-eyes. "Did I ever make you feel good?"

His eyes shifted. He thought for an instant. Then, "Yes. In bed."

"Anyone can be a good fuck," I said.

"Not true," he said. "You made me feel good, but you weren't in love with me. That was hard."

A blond haired, blond toothed, bippy, built boy appeared at our table. Michael introduced his friend Wayne to me. Wayne. Michael's current paramour. Wayne seemed skittish. He and Michael soon departed. Michael left me his new phone number. He wanted to be civilized and keep in touch.

I felt dark. Music played. People continued to dance and get hammered. Rick, the sleaze bag owner of the club was

13

high on ludes when he fell into the chair that Michael had vacated. He asked me if I wanted a blow-job. From him? Why not. Where? His office. I went.

We had no sooner closed his office door when I found my pants and shorts in a heap about my ankles. Rick slobbered all over my crotch. He sucked me, bit me, yanked me until he was winded. I couldn't get hard. He rudely jabbed his finger up my ass, hoping that would provoke a response. I shoved his hand away.

"Don't," I said.

"You got a tight fuckin' hole," he slobbered. He shoved his finger back up in me. "Want me to loosen it up with my cock?"

I didn't want to be there. I wanted to be with you. Again, I removed Rick's hand and yanked up my pants. He started calling me names and stumbled after me. I swung the door shut in his face.

I traversed the dance floor, verbally tacking your description on the forehead of every person I knew, those I remotely knew, then finally strangers. Some had noticed you - then. Not now. You'd once again danced away. Rick appeared on the dance floor, elbowing his way through the people. Mad dog. I wanted a gun. Pop a bullet through his sinus cavity. I quickly scooted along, back out onto the patio. I could hide in the shadows.

The night air was cold. Los Angeles is not the warm, sun filled, plastic town strangers think it is. I had been out there for about two chain smoking hours when I spotted you.

You'd come out for air. Accompanied by a quiet looking fellow. He had a simple, unassuming, yet charming appearance. Someone fresh. Someone sincere. Someone so nauseatingly simple that I was sure he collected ceramic mice from Hallmark. He said something. You laughed. I ached. He huddled into himself and shivered. I saw him refuse your coat. You insisted. He accepted it. With a kiss. You were walking over my face with golf shoes. Sinking the spikes into the bricks I now guarded. You can't do this, I thought. Those acts turn you into a commoner, like me.

Your little friend slid up to you. Wrapped his arms about

14

you. Wanted to dance, there on the patio. Romantic moonlight and rubbish. The fucked little eunuch. I smiled a little when you resisted doing the flagstone waltz. Your little friend coated himself on you. You seemed to like that for you caressed his back as if he were an insinuating cat. Go ahead, I thought. Go to his house. Have him. He'll run you ragged. Chase you down with adamant phone calls and letters signed with smiley faces.

An angry hand grabbed hold of my collar bone. I craned around. Rick stood behind me, the quaaludes popping out of his eyes.

"Hey, babe," he drooled. "Got a horsedick for ya . . ." He grabbed my hand and shoved it into his open fly. "Just play with it . . ." His dick was hard. Pulsing. I started to squeeze it - hard. He moaned. Released my hand. I took it back.

"Not here," I said. He just sneered. He caught me under the arms and pushed me along, back into the club.

As we moved past a few table sitters, Rick swung an arm about my shoulders, holding me like a badger in a trap. I caught sight of Dina talking with some strangers.

"Dina!" I called.

She turned. "Where've you been?! We're ready to go!"

"He don' wanna go yet," Rick said.

"He has to," Dina said. "You can play with him later." She yanked me away from Rick. I blew him a kiss. He flipped me off with a grossly over exaggerated gesture. We met up with Jay at the door. He had a Latin gent on his arm.

"This is Elpedio," Jay said.

"Hi," I said. He grinned and nodded.

"He doesn't speak any English," said Jay. Dina sighed.

We walked out to my car at curbside - a Maverick with an exhaust system ready to knock my teeth out. As I let Jay and his date into the car, I spotted your ugly painted pick-up down and across the street. I slapped the keys into Dina's hands.

"Take my car," I said.

"What?"

15

"Take it. I'm staying."

"But how'll you get back?" she asked.

"I'll hitch if I have to," I said.

"You sure?"

"Yes! Go!"

I shut them into the car. Dina reluctantly revved the engine and drove away. Elpedio waved to me through the rear windshield.

Once they were gone, completely gone, I crossed the street and climbed into the bed of your truck, nestled down and waited.

It seemed like a millennium passed before you showed up - with your little friend, Mr. Toad, in tow. You didn't seem pleased to see me. Your little supplicant became unhinged.

"Who's he?!" the toady shrieked.

"Shut up!" I said.

"Fuck you! Get out of his truck!"

I grabbed Mr. Toad by the hair and yanked him closer. "Got a car for me?" I said.

He sent his claws into my neck. I grabbed his hand and sunk my teeth into it, deeply. He screamed. I released. He looked to you for support. "All right!" the toady said. "Dump him off!"

"You," you said to me. "Climb out." The toady sneered.

"No."

"Then we're going to stay here all night," you said.

"Rex!" Mr. Toad whined.

I looked into the eyes of the slight, little man. "Do you love him?" I said.

"What?" he said.

"Do you love him."

You then looked at your toady. You opened your door and told him to climb in. The doors were shut, keeping me out. We drove off. And drove. All the way to Venice. To a small, ill kept apartment on Horizon Avenue. You both ignored me as you went into the complex. The ocean air intensified the cold of the night. Night, hell. It was almost four in the morning. Was this your place? Or his? Who did

16

I know in Venice that I could drop in on at four am.? A classmate who lived on Dudley. There was a co-worker rooming over on Rose.

How stupid I was. You'd chosen him. Not me. Him. Fine. I was the ass. I climbed out of the pick-up and walked. Walked far. To a pay phone. Who could I call? Who would I not piss off? Who would understand?

Forty minutes later, Jill pulled up in Sue's Falcon. I climbed in. We drove in silence to the Ships restaurant on La Cienega. Mucho coffee was needed.

Jill returned from the cigarette machine with a fresh pack. Real coffee steamed in front of us.

"I was right," she said.

"I'm sorry," I said.

"So am I."

"How'd you know?" I asked.

"I didn't. I just suspected . . ." she said. "We're the same type of creature."

"No gloating?"

"I was," she said, "but I changed my mind. You didn't gloat over Dan."

We talked until 6:30. Talked. And laughed. As we used to. She'd missed our rows. I'd missed her. We drove back to her house. Sat in the living room eating crackers and stale popcorn. Slugging down Diet Pepsi. Maul lounged next to me on the sofa, her enormous mass hogging the space. It felt good.

"Why?" I finally asked.

"Why what?"

"You told me back then to forget him. Why?"

She shrugged. "Fear, maybe. Don't listen to me . . ." she said. We parted with a hug and a kiss. I walked home. Not a thought of you in my head. Things were returning to normal.

As I rounded the corner of Hoover and 32nd Streets, I saw it. That pick-up. Your damned truck in front of my house. I turned and walked the blocks over to Orchard Street to collect my car from Dina.

She made the expected inquiries. I said little, except that

17

I'd scored that night. She let it go. The less who knew of my idiocy, the better. I wound around the blocks, prolonging the short drive back to my place. Then the absurdity of my actions swelled in my head. I drove back home and parked. Right behind your truck. I went into the house. Up the stairs. Into the living room. No one was there. I went back through the kitchen and into my bedroom. You were there. You. In my bed. Your clothes in a heap on the floor. Kurt, I knew, had let you in.

"Why?" I asked.

You turned away from me. Stared at the wall. I went into the bathroom. Stripped. Showered. Shaved my face. Scrubbed my mouth. You wouldn't wait forever, I thought.

When I returned, with a towel about my waist and a pile of smokey clothes in my hands, I found you still there. Vicious people don't cry. I wanted to. My throat felt as if I'd up-chucked a rasp. You turned to face me.

"Why?" you asked.

"I'm incapable of loving. Go home."

"What about being loved?"

A nervous laugh unhitched the clog that had been forming in my throat. "You're not real," I said.

"Maybe not. I'm not sure myself."

I deposited my clothes into the hamper, slamming down the lid for feeble effect, then started picking up stray articles and putting them in their proper places.

"What happened with your friend," I said.

"Nothing," you said. "Who brought you home?"

"Jill," I said.

"Oh," you said. I wanted to dive into that bed with you, but couldn't. "I came back out for you," you said, "but you'd gone."

"Did you," I said. "I made an ass out of myself tonight and yet you took that toady home. I'd waited in that truck for hours."

"Twenty minutes."

"Whatever!" I said. "It seemed to me that your decision had been made. Mr. Toad - Yes. Me - No!" I slammed the closet door shut. The window glass rattled. "Why are you

18

doing this to me?!"

"Doing what?"

"Come in, then run out! Come in, then run out! Off! On! Off! Gone! Back on! You make me crazier than even I thought I could get! Shit! I don't even know your last name!"

"It's Reynolds," you said.

"Well that's a fine fuckin' how do you do!"

Silence. For a moment. You in my bed. Me out of it.

"Was it all happenstance?" I asked.

"Nothing really is."

"That party on Menlo," I said. "Who invited you?"

"I invited myself."

"You wanted to take me home that night," I said.

"I did."

"Why?"

"I wanted to," you said.

My legs were tired from being up forever. I wanted to lie down. I sat on the floor instead.

"What're you afraid of?" you asked.

"You," I said. "You'll leave again."

"And yet I'll come back."

"Don't," I said. "I can't . . ."

"Talk with me," you said. "Here, in bed." You pulled the covers back. Inviting me in. All the way in. I weakened. I went to you. As I slid in next to you, I became erect. I felt your hand remove my towel. It fell by the wayside, a discarded wrapper. My stomach muscles contracted painfully when you touched me. God, keep me from losing myself to you.

You propped yourself up on an elbow and stared at me. Studied my face. I felt my throat closing again. Choking. The apple scent. Subtle. Your hands, never touching but hovering a scant shadow above my skin, explored me. My body bristled with a static foreign charge. I fought not to cry, to not let you slip between the now cracking masonry in me. You must've blown the horn at Jericho, I thought, for my walls were caving in. You guided me to you, to press my numbed flesh against yours. And I melted. The

19

ice berg struck the Titanic and I was sinking. Into your chest, your arms, underarms, inhaling you, devouring you. Neck to nipples, oval and dark. Sweetmeat. Cupping your buttocks as your hands rasped over my thighs, kneading the muscles, then moved up to my ass. I moved my mouth down, licking every cell of flesh in my way, down to your navel, the soft hair of your crotch. You pulled my groin to your face. Licking, nibbling, nursing all around my swollen cock. All around. I pressed my face between your thighs, savouring your odour. The taste of your balls, your rosette hole, probing into you with my tongue. My testicles slid in and out of your mouth. I could feel your nose, your eyelashes brush the base of my cock as your finger, wet with your spit, pressed between my ass cheeks, into my rectum. All was beyond bliss for me. You were this rogue cannibal's feast. I ate you. I sucked you. Licked you. Loved you with a voraciousness I'd never experienced. The pleasure was painful, until I could endure it no longer. I wanted you in me. All the way in. As our tongues once again met, I leaned back onto your shaft. We eased you into me. You were now me. The one union people fantasise about. The perfect oneness. For hours we remained in that bed, exploring, then re-exploring each other until not a molecule of flesh remained unattended. God, keep me from losing myself . . . to you. God denied this hedonist's prayer. I was lost.

A deep slumber ensued. Your heartbeat talked into my ear. Reassuring me. Securing me. I loved you.

We awoke at ten that night. The stubble on your face had filled out more. You smelled like sex. Sex has a peculiar smell. People can often identify it, but never quite describe it. I liked smelling it on you. On me. A husky scent. We made love again. This time you allowed me into you. I was happy. Honestly happy. The sensation of your body feeling pleasure made me high. I wanted you to feel good. To feel beyond good. Your panting mouth exhaling your euphoric orgasm down my throat as we kissed. Your racing heart, your tightening muscles, your chest and cheeks burning crimson. I came. In you. Left part of myself in you. And your expulsion - human honey - welded us together. We slept again.

✳ ✳ ✳ ✳ ✳

Though the window shades were drawn, darkened with age and nicotine, the morning intruded into the room. I wanted to paint a portrait of you as you were, peaceful in your slumber. To keep you still, there with me, forever. Death is forever. I'd read somewhere of a religion that subscribed to the belief of a life after death wherein people were reborn into a world, a world in which the inhabitants spent eternity making love on green chaise lounges in the woods. Unions for time ever after. I could spend that time with you.

You stirred a bit, nestled into yourself and drifted off again. A comfortable sleep. I was afraid to move, to learn your disappearing pattern hadn't changed. You loved me, I knew. You'd given yourself to me. Would you want breakfast? Would you want to make love again? Would you want to leave? I could make no assumptions. I had to shower. Had to tend to responsibilities already prescribed for the day. I ran my hands over my body, pressing my flesh hard, wanting to embed your smell into me. I had to shower.

Soap felt like acid removing an indelible mark. I hated that shower. It robbed your scent from my present. I felt like a mannequin. A human form without human depth. I shaved. Polished the teeth. Forced life into my hair. A walking advertisement of what "image makers" tout as "the image." Clean, clean, clean and hollow to the core.

I didn't want to leave the bathroom. You'd be gone, I thought. Kurt knocked on the door. He wanted in. I had to come out.

You were gone. The bed was empty. I felt a nausea churn in my stomach. I slowly took in the room, my eyes scanning for an arm, a shoe, a thigh, anything that was you. Nothing.

Through the house, the entire house, I looked in vain. Without a trace, as they say. Again. Outside. No pick-up truck. Again. Gone again.

21

I resolved at that moment to return to a non-feeling life. I made breakfast for Kurt, for me. I invited Jill and Sue, Dina, Laurie and Jay. Eggs, bacon, ham steaks, French toast, toast butter, jam, coffee. Enough food to stop ten hearts. We drank Mimosas, Bloody Marys and Salty Dogs. Everyone thought it a wonderfully decadent foodfest. They all laughed and prattled on and on.

I ate. I watched. I laughed at their lunacy. Carry on, they say, and I did. When it was all said and done, I cleared the plates from the table and carried them into the kitchen. I ran water. Scalding water. Filled the sink with steam and suds. Jill came in just as I slammed the stack of plates into the water.

"Those aren't yours to break," she said.

"Some are."

She pulled out a plate. "Yours?" I nodded. She stuck the plate in my hand. "This," she said, "is his heart."

I smashed the plate over the edge of the counter. Two-thirds of it littered the floor. Jill looked at the pieces. She chose a fragment - a small fragment - took away the piece that I still clung to, then pressed the tiny piece into the palm of my hand, closing my fingers about it.

"Keep this piece," she said. "Carry it with you at all times. When you see him again, and you will, pull this piece from your pocket and remember today."

"I'm trying to forget."

"Forgetting is impossible." She pulled up a chain that was hiding beneath her blouse. A small pendant of red glass, set in gold, hung between her fingers. "This was a gift once. A Valentine of carnations in red glass. The flowers didn't even have time to die. I remember. We all remember."

I had never seen it before. An odd fraction of red nothing set in precious gold.

"Did you feel dead?" I asked.

"We all feel dead. You know that."

I found a whisk broom and swept up his shattered heart. Jill popped open a beer. The others continued to laugh in the dining room. Jill's gaze drifted to the closed kitchen door. Watching. Them. Through the wood barrier. Listening. Motionless. I finished my task. Burying the wreckage into a brown paper bag beneath the sink.

"Come on . . ." she said, as if speaking of the others, waiting for them to dispense a bit of prime gossip.

"What?"

"You," she said. "Come on." She set down her beer, grabbed my hand and led me out the back door.

The daylight was harsh. We moved down the grayed wood stairs to the driveway, then out to the street, to my car.

"Drive," she said.

"Where?"

"Venice."

✻ ✻ ✻ ✻ ✻

We had to park a good many blocks from your street. A weekend at the beach translates into a crash of cars parked bumper on bumper.

"This is it?" Jill asked as we stood in the alleyway behind your - or his - building.

"They came here."

Jill swung open the gate and ascended the stairs. I followed, not knowing what she intended on doing. We entered a hallway on a second floor.

"Which one?" she asked. I shrugged. Hadn't been inside the building. There were four doors. She knocked on one. A frail woman answered. No prize. She knocked next door. I recognized the voice.

"Who is it?" Mr. Toad's voice whined.

"Jill," said Jill.

The door opened a crack. "Jill?" said the toady. "I don't know an . . ."

"You stay the fuck away from, Rex, qweebman!" she said.

"Go fuck yourself!" shrieked the toady.

Big mistake. Jill slammed against the door. It flew open. I heard Mr. Toad crash land. Jill disappeared inside. Her mouth flew. Acid splattered. I was sure Mr. Toad had taken his final wild ride. I moved to the doorway. Peered in. She

23

loomed over him. Screaming. His walls were adorned with Judy Garland paraphernalia. A true queen.

Jill pivoted and marched out of the apartment. Mr. Toad spotted me as I followed her. He wanted to peel my face.

As we moved down the stairs, it struck me - the apple scent. It was in my nose. I turned back. Back up the stairs. Jill, confused, stopped and watched me go. Back. In there. Toady was righting an overturned coffee table. I could smell it. Apples.

"Hey!" he hissed. "I'm calling the cops you stupid fucking fuck head!"

I found my way into the bedroom. The bed was unmade. Two people had slept there. I picked up the pillows. Inhaled deeply. You. Your smell was on one of them.

"He's not here," Mr. Toad said. We stared at each other a moment. He came closer, deflated, exhausted. "He was here. Came by this morning."

"And?"

"He slept. We slept. Independent sleep," he said as he sank on the bed.

"And now?"

Mr. Toad turned to me, his face sullen - lonely. That said enough. I stroked his hair.

"I don't know," he said. "I wish I did."

"Do you love him?"

"There's no point because there's no such thing."

I gripped his shoulder. A reassuring, sympathetic touch. "Sorry . . ." I said. I left him alone.

I joined Jill back on the stairs. "I apologize to you, to him," I said.

She sighed an understanding sigh. "Maybe you should forget . . ."

"I can't."

"I know . . ." she said. "Let's go get a beer."

* * * * *

There was a buzz of activity along the beach. Vendors, gawkers. Selling, buying. Skaters, musclemen, vagrants, everyone - out to see and be seen.

24

Sun melts beer drinkers. We were as lifeless as the plastic molded chairs in which we sat. My face burned from sunlight. A crinkly burn. My nose would fall off any moment. Two empty pitchers on the table. One a third full. A clogged ashtray to one side. To walk would be to slosh, yet I didn't feel full.

A young man on skates crashed through the crowd of people and dogs congesting the street. An abrupt halt. At our table. Glass clinked.

"Sorry . . ." he said.

"Are you?" Jill said.

"Yeah," he said.

"Who're you anyway?" she asked, her sunglasses hiding her red eyes.

"Taylor."

"Jill. Can you bake a cherry pie?"

"No," he said.

"Good," she said. "I hate cherry pie."

"Sit," I said.

"Do you hate cherry pie, too?" he asked.

"Hate all pie, save peach," I said. He sat.

"You just hangin'?" he asked.

I pushed my glass towards him. "You old enough to drink?"

"No," he said.

"Neither are we," I said.

He filled the glass with warm beer and drank. Jill lit another cigarette, coughed, puffed. He was a thin fellow, maybe eighteen - near, very near our age. Dirty blond hair bleaching cleaner from the sun. A tank top and shorts exposed his thin frame.

"Locals?" he asked.

"God no," said Jill.

"Me neither," he said. "I'd like to be but I can't afford it."

"Where do you live?" Jill asked.

"Hollywood. You?"

"Near Downtown," she said.

"Ah," he said. "SC brats."

"Not brats," she said. "Daddy don't pay our bills."

25

"Who then?"

"Loans and scholarships," she said. "And work."

"Do you talk?" he said to me.

"When I've something to say."

He chewed a swallow of beer, sighed and looked around at the passers-by. "Neptune's moving out of Scorpio and into Capricorn," he said. "Know what that means?" We didn't. "Means the party's gonna be over soon."

"When does this happen?" I asked.

"In the early eighties. I hope to be in Amsterdam by then."

"Bully," said Jill. "Bully." She then shoved her glass toward him for a refill.

"Drink to Neptune," he said.

"Just drink," she said.

"What do you do?" I said.

"Awk . . ." he said, his eyes averting mine. "I'm a free agent."

"Free agents usually have a specific trade," Jill said.

"Gotta do a lot of things," he said. "Why are you two hangin' out here?"

"Because we don't drive BMW's," she said. He liked that answer. He chugged the rest of the beer and belched. Jill cracked a smile. She like crass actions. Taylor removed his skates.

"You hustle?" I asked.

"I do what I gotta do."

"We're heading back," Jill said. "Want to come?"

Taylor thought for a moment then shrugged. He'd nothing better planned.

We walked back to my car in silence. Jill led, then me, then Taylor with his skates slung over his shoulder. We piled into the Maverick and drove down Lincoln Boulevard to Highway 10 - the 10 to locals. It was 55 taken at 65 and riding the line all the way to Hoover, then to Jill's. We got there in one piece. Went in. Connie and Maul were on the sofa watching an old western on television.

"Brian called," Connie said. "Call him back."

We went upstairs to Sue's room. Sue was on her bed,

reading.

"Hey," she said. "Brian called. Call him."

"Fuck Brian," Jill said. "Sue, this is Taylor."

"Hey, Taylor," she said. Taylor nodded. "Where'd you guys disappear to? Kurt wouldn't clean up the place without you."

"He'll live," I said.

"See?" Jill said to Taylor. "No designer nada. Poor people do attend private schools."

"Guess so," said Taylor. The phone rang. Jill crossed into her room to answer it.

"Brian," Sue said. "She's going to be on with him all night. Sit."

I flopped onto the bed. Maul entered the room, sniffed Taylor like an afterthought in her dog dish, then climbed onto the bed.

"Bed hog," said Sue as she shifted to make way for the Dane.

"Did you guys have a good time?" I asked, not really caring.

"Yeah, 'til Jay got horny. Clark dropped by. He and Clark went into your room to screw. The rest of us went home. Where'd you go?"

"To the beach."

She looked at Taylor. "And you?"

"I crashed into their table."

"Oh," she said as she flipped a page in her book. She looked at Taylor again. "You going to sit, or what?" Taylor sat on the edge of the bed, keeping himself as small as possible. "Why'd you go to the beach," she said.

"Just to look."

"For him?"

"We found a wormy apple," I said.

Jill came back into the room wearing a smile. "Brian's coming over."

I knew what that meant. Good-bye. She'd been hung up on Brian for months. He wasn't like Dan. Didn't hang with our crowd. She didn't like to share him with us. I accepted that. I didn't want to share - you - with anyone.

27

"Call me tomorrow," I said, pecking her cheek. "I've class straight through, then work. I'll be in at eleven."

Taylor followed me down the stairs and out the door. The air had turned cool. Taylor shivered.

"Hollywood, you said?"

"Yeah," he said. "Sierra Bonita."

We got back on the 10 and headed East. I turned on the heater for him.

"Do you work?" I asked again to dispel the silence.

"Yeah . . ." he said. Then, "You people don't seem happy."

I laughed. "Are you?"

"Not always. But life ain't to be pissed away. Gotta make yourself happy some of the time," he said.

"You're right . . ."

"What makes you happy?"

"Dunno," I said not wanting to mention you.

"I am a hustler," he said slowly.

"Why?"

"'Cause it's what I know."

"And you're happy," I said.

"Not always. But I can make myself feel good at times. I go to Venice. I skate. Pretend I'm someone else. Things like that."

"You ran away?"

"Something like that," he said.

"How old are you?"

"Does it matter?"

"You tell me."

"It doesn't . 'Til ya get too old."

"Then what?" I asked.

"Dunno . . ." he said.

"At least you're honest."

"You're not?" he asked.

"Not even with myself."

"Who burned you?"

"What?"

"Who burned you," he said.

"I burned myself," I said - and I did, with you. Clink-clink. Brick-brick. Keep everyone out.

"We all do that," he said. "That's why I hustle." I turned up Sierra Bonita. "There," he said. "On the left."

I pulled up in front of his house. An aging whitewashed bungalow with a long concrete porch painted a deep, deep red. Fresh blood red. Dead red.

"It's sixty seven years old," he said. The yard was a harvest of foxtails.

"Who else lives here?"

"Others," he said. "We have a rent kitty. Drop in what ya can. Come inside."

The house was dark. Something sad. Something intimidating. It was seven o'clock. I parked the car. We went up to the porch.

"What about the others?" I asked.

"Out."

"How old are you, Taylor?"

"How old are you?"

"Nineteen."

"Seventeen. Got a problem with that?" he said. I shook my head. We went inside.

The house smelled moldy. Brown carpet hid dirt as the light went on. An old sofa, sagging in its centre. Plastic milk crates for end tables. A mattress in the corner. Another in the dining room. Yellowed. Gray with dust.

He led me through the dining room into a bedroom. A nightstand, lamp and queen size bed filled a room otherwise devoid of personality.

"I pay more for the privacy," he said. "The johns I pick up like it better this way."

"You always bring them here?"

"Just the bar trade. The old farts. Most other times it's in their cars." He took off his tank top, exposing his back to me. A long, thick slanted scar branded him. He noticed me staring at it. "Weirdo with a sharpened church key. Wanted blood." The scar was gross on his thin, tanned back. I wanted to touch it.

"Why?" I asked.

"Who the fuck knows? He was into blood and scat. Jack threw him out."

29

"Jack?"

"A guy who used to be here. Got himself knifed last summer screwing some Latin trade. Guy's lover killed 'em both."

"And you find a way to be happy?" I said. He removed his shorts. A boyish ass. Smooth. Small.

"It's what I gotta do to keep my head all in, ya know?" He pulled a joint out of the pocket of a pair of pants heaped on the floor then sat on the bed next to me. "There's a match in the nightstand," he said.

I found the matches and an ashtray - an old tuna can. He lit the joint. Inhaled into tomorrow, then handed it to me. I smoked. We toked. He was erect. A nice cock. A slight sway to the left. I lay back on the bed, feeling light-heavy.

"Wanta fuck me?" he said as he drew up next to me. I did. And I didn't.

"Is that what you want?"

"Sure. Better someone I like, ya know?" He reached into the nightstand for some poppers and a dirty jar of Vaseline. My shoes came off. Then my pants. Shorts. I was erect.

"What makes you feel good?" I said. He straddled my body and fondled my dick.

"Do to me what you like done to you," he said.

I pulled his boyish ass to my face. He resisted a bit. I took a hit of poppers and plunged my face between his ass cheeks, licking, sucking, nuzzling his hole. His body tensed. I bit. He groaned, rubbed Vaseline onto my cock as my tongue, fingers worked his hole.

I did everything to him that night, save fuck him. Everything that gave pleasure to him. I didn't want to fuck. His johns did that. I wanted him to feel good. To feel cared about, cared for. I didn't know if I truly did care but I wanted to. I wanted him to feel for me as I had felt for you. I was you. He was me. I had no thoughts of you at that time.

We were in each others arms, his head heavy on my chest, when we heard the front door slam. Taylor sat up with a start. Voices. He jumped up and tossed me my clothes.

"Go!" he said.

"Wha . . .?"

"Taylor!!!" the voice shot out. A violent call. I jumped into my pants. He knocked open the window. Before I knew what was happening, I was outside the house, barefoot in the damp weeds. I stepped into my shoes. I heard the bedroom door slam open.

"Fuckin' fuckhead fuckup!!!" the man yelled. A big man. Dark. Greek. Maybe Middle-Eastern. He backhanded Taylor. A shuttlecock shot across the room.

"Fuckin' rippin' me off!!! Ya didn't make my drop!" The man slugged Taylor.

I ran alongside the house and out to the street. I jumped into the car. How do you stop it? In there? I pressed into the horn. Let it blast. Blasted it 'til the neighbours came out screaming and the cops arrived.

I stated what I saw to the policeman. They entered the house. They came back shortly, angry. No one complained. No one but that man inside. No kid. They were going to cite me for disturbing the peace. I threatened to call the papers, the television, took their badge numbers and threatened to fight them and sue them and the city when they found Taylor dead. I was lucky they let me go.

I stayed away that night. Thinking of him. Of you. Taylor was someone who might stay with me if his past didn't pull him away - permanently. You though, you chose departure. To remain unknown. I'd read the paper tomorrow for Taylor's obituary.

I didn't have time to read the paper. Classes cut through a bleary eyed day. Then work. Boring work. Orders. Tips. Orders. Orders. The glamorous life of a waiter.

Jill called that night. Another party on Menlo Street. She with Brian, me with - whomever I wanted to bring. And she was opening in a show at the Stop Gap Theatre. Come and see.

I stayed in that night, a Monday night. Homework until two in the morning. College equals papers. Short papers. Long papers. And tests. Many, many tests. The rite of passage into the world, they say. Whose world. Perhaps I would've had better luck with alchemy. Did anyone really care about Tulipomania in 17th Century The Netherlands?

31

Or that Los Angeles will move up to where San Francisco is in X million of years? Or that Hercules was reported to have had a hairy ass? One learns weird shit in college. To be well rounded, they say. Bah. I was to meet Jill at one o'clock the next day at Mudd Hall on campus.

I tried to sleep but thought of Taylor. I wanted to go back to his bungalow. Find him. Play saviour. Be God to someone. I could look good. Feel superior. Who was I kidding?

✳ ✳ ✳ ✳ ✳

One o'clock turned into two o'clock before Jill showed up. I'd hunkered up under the portico against the brick wall, studying the old courtyard. She was smiling when she called to me.

"I'm sorry," she said. "Rehearsal ran late."

"What's the play?"

"Mother Courage."

"Brecht," I said.

"Anyhow . . ." she said.

"So?"

"What happened?"

"I took him home. We did it. Slept a bit, then his pimp or whatever burst in and knocked him about like a handball."

"What?!"

"Do you have a newspaper?" I asked.

"What?!" she said again. "You left him?!"

"I want to see if he's dead."

She hit me. "That's sick!"

I got up. "I called the damn cops! They didn't do anything!" I said then moved out towards University Avenue. She trailed.

"Is he dead?! Is he dead?!" she said.

"I don't know."

"And people call me an insensitive bitch!" she said. "I can't believe you!"

"Look," I said as I stopped, "call me what you want, but I couldn't do anything short of getting the police there that wouldn't have put me six feet under in a pine box! Okay?!"

32

I started walking again. She followed. We walked down to the Commons, aka The Ptomaine Palace. "Sorry," she said.

"How's Brian?"

"Great. And a shit," she said.

"Won't play games, will he?" She shook her head. "Yeah, I know. It's like trying to read a book in Greek when you've only studied French."

"Tu voudrais boire du café?" she asked.

"Smart-ass," I said. "Oui."

* * * * *

We sat at the concrete picnic tables at the rear of the Commons building. A quiet spot along a little used sidewalk. She'd put fake creamer into her coffee. It turned the colour of his truck. Your truck.

"What is it?" she asked, stirring chemical sweetener into the unappetizingly coloured coffee.

I gave a slight shake of the head. A shrug. Lit a cigarette. "Nothing." A pigeon swooped down from the roof to salvage a stale piece of pizza on a nearby table. It shit on the concrete bench. "What are we doing?"

"Drinking coffee."

"With our lives. Taylor said we didn't seem happy."

"Getting knocked around by a pimp doesn't seem like happiness to me. Who's he to talk."

"Are you?" I asked.

She sipped her coffee, grimaced at the taste, then cleared her throat. "We've only been alive about twenty years. A lot of shit has happened in those years . . ."

True. Memories of childhood. A television screen. Miss Mary Ann of Romper Room being cut off. The breaking story - President Kennedy's assassination. I was about four. Almost five. Kids always like to be older. My mother on the phone. People coming in and out. My brother being sent home from school, telling me I'm a dummy 'cause I didn't know what was going on. The beginning. Newscasts of a war in a jungle country. Weird names. Teenagers politicking to younger kids. Parents, elders politicking to younger kids. Do drugs. Don't. Don't have sex. Do. Fuck

33

the commie bastard pinko bullshit useless idiots in the ass. Bomb a college in the name of God. My hometown, Santa Cruz. Near Fort Ord. Near San Francisco. Metaphysics. God. Family. Extended family. Summer of Love floating up the coastline. Communal everything. It's all wrong. They're all wrong. Years of it. Johnson, Leary, Angela Davis, Joni Mitchell, Martha Mitchell, free love and anarchy in the military and I haven't a clue what to think 'cause you say they're wrong, they say you're wrong. No one's right for more than a decade. Stay zoned out. Don't listen. Fuck 'til you're dead. Fuck to keep from feeling dead. Sex is left. Right or wrong. Sex is left. All is contrary. It was one hell of a time to grow up, the 60's.

"Well?" she said.

"You're right. Nobody taught us how to be happy."

"Rex makes you happy."

"Only when he's around." She didn't pursue it. "We're going to the Odessy tonight. You coming?"

She shook her head. "Don't like the place. Besides, I'm seeing Brian."

"Ah," I said. "He wouldn't like the place."

"He might," she said wryly. "He likes to dance. I don't want him there, though. All those guys would end up hitting on him."

I nodded. "It's the Odessy, then Studio One, then the Mother Lode."

She looked at her watch. "Got a class in twenty minutes. Women and Men in Society. A real snooze." We rose and headed off in the direction of Founder's Hall.

"It's a puzzle," she said.

"What is?"

"Figuring out how little, or how much it's going to take for us to find out what 'happy' is supposed to be."

I stopped. The trees looked lost against the smoggy backdrop of a sky. "I gotta run, too," I said. Gave her a peck on the cheek and continued on to Jefferson Boulevard toward home.

✳ ✳ ✳ ✳ ✳

I found Kurt rummaging through my desk drawer. He held up a cheque. "Trading for cash," he said. I kept a stash of tip money in my drawer. Friends sometimes cashed small cheques in my make-shift till if they didn't want to wait in the cheque cashing line at 32nd Street Market.

"Fine," I said.

"Clark gave Jay the clap," he said.

"He noticed it in two days?"

"That's what he says. They're not speaking."

"You coming with us tonight?" I asked.

"No," he said. "There's an old movie on television tonight. June Lockhart's in it. Dina and I are going to be glued to the glass."

"All right."

"Jay said he'd pick you up at eight."

I nodded. He left. I shut the door and flopped on the bed. I dozed off for a time. A dreamless sleep. A finger prodded into my side like a thumb tack being pressed into tin. Kurt was hovering over me.

"Sue's on the phone," he said. "She says it's important."

* * * * *

She said Taylor was at her house and that I should come collect him. All right. Sure. I hung up the telephone and went.

* * * * *

His left eye. Bruised. Turning black. His lip. Swollen. Split. Brown red with dried blood. As soon as he saw me he tried to smile. Brown red turned vivid red. Again he was in a tank top and shorts. The same articles of clothing I met him in. Sue came out of the kitchen with a fresh compress.

"Hey," she said to me as she handed him the compress. He dabbed his swollen eye, then dabbed it against his lip.

"Your friend?" I asked him. He nodded.

"I gotta find someplace else to stay," he said. Sue shot me a 'please don't even ask me' look. I didn't.

"Come on," I said.

"Gotta use the can first."

35

"It's through the kitchen," Sue said. He went. She turned back to me. "Do you know what happened?"

"I can guess. He's a hustler."

"Oh," she said. Pause. "Aren't you adopting a problem?"

"Problems come and go," I said.

"You trust him?" she asked, her tone implying I shouldn't.

"Don't have a choice," I said.

The echo of pipes flushing. Slllwooosh. He came back out. "I left the rag on the edge of the tub," he said. "Thanks . . ."

"Sure," Sue said. I nodded good-by. She nodded back. We left.

"How come you didn't talk to the police that night?" I asked.

"Fahad locked me in the closet. Said he'd throw a live rat in with me if I made a sound."

"There are halfway houses, Social Service . . ." I said.

"Fuck that!" he said.

"Why?"

"I'll be eighteen in May. Then what? They turn me back out onto the street."

We pulled up in front of my house. Jay's car was there. We went in. As we ascended the stairs, I heard Jay expounding on his version of catching the clap. He shut up when he saw Taylor. Gave me a kiss, then extended his hand and a smile to my charge.

"Jay," he said.

"Taylor." Taylor shook his hand.

"What happened to you?" he asked.

"Long story," I said. Then to Taylor, "My room's back through the kitchen, across from the bathroom." Taylor nodded meekly to Jay, then to Kurt and Dina who were seated on the couch ready and waiting for the June Lockhart flick to hit the boob tube, then he went on.

"Who's he?" Kurt asked.

"A friend," I said. "Jay, I don't think I'm going to make it tonight."

"I'll wait," he said. He wanted to meet Taylor. I could tell. He was permanently horny. "Bars don't get going 'til at least ten o'clock, anyhow."

"Naw," I said. "You go ahead. Give me a call around nine-thirty. Maybe we'll catch up with you."

He shrugged. "All right." He said his good-byes and left. Dina had a look of consternation on her face.

"How come he's here?" she asked, expecting a straight answer.

"Because he hasn't anywhere else to go that I know of," I said. Kurt scowled.

"You just gonna leave him here?" he said.

"If I go, he'll go with me! Okay?! Jesus Christ!" I stormed back to my room. Taylor was sitting on the bed. He had heard them.

"Sorry . . ." he said. His voice cracked. Close to crying. He defied it. "You got plans for tonight?"

"Go take a shower," I said. "I'll find some clothes for you."

He went into the bathroom. When I heard the water running, I went to the kitchen to try to pull together something resembling food. Spaghetti. Filling. Cheap. Quick. Handy. Everyone has a package of spaghetti and a can of tuna on hand.

Leaving the pot of water on to boil, I went back and randomly selected a shirt - Oxford, white, and jeans - faded, shrunken a little too much for me.

I slopped some very done pasta onto a plate, smothered it in sauce, gathered up utensils, a glass of milk and some bread. Into my room with it. Onto the desk. He was fastening the last two buttons on the shirt.

"Bread's a little stale," I said. He didn't mind. He wolfed down the pasta. I watched him eat. He didn't seem to mind me watching him eat. He cleaned the plate with the bread. I played waiter. Dropped the plate into the sink. It clanked against the porcelain, spin-wobbled, then settled. Fingers felt in pockets. Fished it out. That piece of shattered plate. The piece of your heart.

"Got any toothpaste?" he asked, sawing dental floss through his teeth. He looked like he'd slipped into a robe. Something comfortable. Something easy. I sent him back to the bathroom with instructions for oral hygiene. He found me back in the bedroom.

"What am I going to do with you?" I said.

"Don't gotta do anything," he said. "I'll go."

"Sit," I said. He sat. "Want to go back out there?" He shook his head. "You ever bus tables?" He shook his head. "You're going to learn then." He shook his head. "Why not?"

"'Cause no one's gonna hire me," he said.

"My boss will. He's cheap. You get tips from the waitstaff if you do a good job."

"And where'm I supposed to live?"

"Here," I said. "For awhile."

"Your roommate won't like that."

"So, we'll adjust his rent. Come on. We're going out."

✳ ✳ ✳ ✳ ✳

The Odessy was crowded. Rick, aka Asshole, didn't question Taylor's age. He was too busy snarling at me. I figured that Jay would eventually show up here.

Taylor's eyes were wide, swallowing the lights that pulsed with the beat of the music, like a man dropped onto another planet. I took his arm and lead him back through the bar and out onto the patio. The open air gas fire burned yellow-blue in its pit.

"You okay?"

"Yeah," he said. "Never been here before. Usually the Rusty Nail or the Blue Parrot. Got lots of johns at the Parrot."

"This is a club."

"Yeah," he said. He didn't really care. I could tell. Novelty worn off in ten seconds flat, this place was just another place like any other place like any other trick in any other bar.

We drank juice outside. Didn't say much. Just watched people meander in and out, in and out. An endless cycle of people looking for someone - specific - in general. Some nodded to me. I replied likewise. Michael, my ex, came out onto the flagstone perch. Michael, sans a bippy blond boy. He smiled at Taylor as he said hello to me. Catch us on the

38

dance floor later, I said and sent him on his way.

"He's cute," Taylor said.

"He's nice," I said. "Nicely nice."

"Wanta dance?"

People packed butt to butt to crotch to crotch to butt again. Bottles of Locker Room, Rush, Bolt - poppers - floated freely about. Occasionally an ether soaked rag, a remnant of the early 70's, swung into mouths to be teethed on. Chew and inhale. Pump, pump, pump. The heart. The blood. Dizzying. Erections strained against zipper locked cloth. Neptune's influence. Bodies dripped orgasmic sweat. The answer to everything - feel it all.

"Headache?" I asked. He nodded. "Want to go?" He did. I didn't.

"You do this all the time?" he asked. I nodded. "Why?"

"What else is there? I work. I study. I go crazy being at home."

"Why?"

"Why what?"

"Why do you go crazy being at home?"

"It's lonely," I said with a shrug.

"I like being alone," he said. "No one gives you shit."

"How do you feel now?"

"Better. Your friends never showed."

"They're probably at the 8709," I said. "Or the YMAC."

"I lived, sometimes, at the Club Baths," he said. "I could always get some sleep there."

"Why'd you leave home? He shifted. Awkward. Uncomfortable. Silent. "Where's home?"

"Bakersfield," he said. I waited for further information. It didn't come. "Why do you go crazy being alone?"

I lit a cigarette. He stared. Continued to stare. Wait. Why should I give a response? He didn't. I could feel a popper burn blistering under my nostrils. Great, I thought. An oozy crusty healing process. I pulled a tube of ointment out of my pocket - technically goo for chapped lips - and slathered it under my snout.

"Get some Neosporin," he said.

"Doesn't come in vending machines."

"We can go to the store," he said. I didn't say anything. "You're tired of this place. Let's go."

Down La Cienega Boulevard, to the 10, to Hoover Street. Los Angeles was full of 24 hour supermarkets. Everything from danish to drugs. Legal drugs. I paid for the ointment and smeared it under my nose before I got back into the car. Taylor had waited. I climbed into the car and revved the engine. Parking lot lights and purple black air blended. Taylor was staring straight ahead. His cock jutted out from his open fly. I bent over and wrapped my mouth around him. He tensed, then gently pulled my head back. He loosely tucked himself back into his pants.

"Why'd you do that?"

"I'm sorry," he said. "I shouldn't have done it."

We drove back in silence, went up to my room in silence, got into my bed in silence. He wouldn't say and I wouldn't ask.

It was about three in the morning. I was aware that neither one of us was asleep.

"Why'd you push me away?" I asked. Taylor sighed. "Okay, don't talk."

He propped himself up on an elbow. "I was wrong," he said. "But, I got scared."

"Of what?"

"That you were tired of me." He leaned back and stared at the ceiling. "Everybody else is."

Tired of him, I thought. No. Not tired. Lie. I was tired. Like you were of me. In the short time I knew this young man who lay next to me, I realized he'd done one thing. He made me forget about you, even if only until now.

Taylor's hand slid under the waistband of my briefs, each finger crawling through the hair, down to my cock. I didn't understand him. First yes, then no. My body responded to his touch. My hand pressed his groin. Through the white cotton I felt his hardness again. The tip of his penis poked out from under his shorts, the elastic waist choking its full head. My fingers pushed the waistband down so that it caught beneath his balls, forcing them to ride up high, swollen.

"What makes you lonely?" he asked.

I slid down and took the length of his cock down my throat. He didn't push me away. I continued up and down, sucking him hard, then lightly. His body trembled, but not so much as a gasp came out of him. He tried to caress my face, shoulders, any part of me that he could touch. I pushed his hands away until he finally stopped trying. He came in spasms. I let his withering organ slide from between my lips. He sobbed quietly.

"What?" I said. He rolled over towards the wall. I sighed and lay back watching a swirl of shadows on the ceiling. I was tired. Too tired to sleep. Too tired not to. "Please don't cry . . ." I said without looking at him. "I'm in love. That's why I'm lonely."

He rolled back to me. "With who?"

"Someone . . ." I said.

"I don't think I've been in love," he said.

"But," I said, "that's what you want."

"I guess so."

"There's a difference," I said. "We don't make love, we have sex."

"Who is he?"

"Just someone . . ." We lay quiet for a time, then he leaned over, kissed my forehead and nestled down by my side to sleep. God, I thought, I'm in love with the invisible man and I've a needy, responsive young hustler by my side needing to be loved. Fuck it. Bring on more cement. Bring on the bricks.

✱ ✱ ✱ ✱ ✱

I gave Taylor a spare set of keys to the house, much to Kurt's disdain, and got him a job bussing tables at the restaurant. He worked hard, often pulling double shifts. He wanted a way out. He moved from my bed to the floor. His choice. Where I continued on with Jill, Sue and the rest of my group, Taylor picked up new acquaintances and friends through the restaurant. After a month or so, Kurt finally got fed up with the third roommate and decided to move out. I never saw or heard from you again during that time. No matter how often I went out, no matter where I

41

went to, you were gone.

Finals wound down. Summer was coming. Jill invited everyone over for a bar-b-que - a sort of birthday bar-b-que for Jay and Taylor. I hadn't seen Jill as much as she had yet another boyfriend. A very agreeable man named Steven.

All the old gang gathered, though Jay and Clark were still cool towards each other because of the clap incident. Jill pulled me into the house to help with the final food preparations. Steaks and burger patties, green salads, potato salad, two quiches and garnish. And one large chocolate cake.

"Got enough," I said.

"Steve and I were at the 502 Club last night," she said as she fought to unstick a ball of non-stick cling wrap. "Rex was there with some woman."

"That's no longer my business," I said.

"He asked how you were."

"That's nice."

Jill looked at me for a moment. It was the kind of look one gets when one's debating whether or not to share some sordid secret. She picked up her purse off the counter, dug around in it, then handed me a matchbook. "His number's inside." I just stared at it. Didn't want to take it. She stuck it in my shirt pocket. I then dug in my pants pocket for my scrap of plate. I held it up to her.

"Remember this?" I said. "You said it was his heart."

She shrugged. "Life goes on, though, doesn't it?" She picked up the tray of meat and headed outside. "Bring the salads."

I pulled out the matchbook. A number. A name. Your name. My gut wanted me to call you right then and there. My head said don't. I picked up the salad bowls and went outside.

Smoke billowed from the bar-b-que. Everyone, dressed in spring attire, sipped from glasses and bottles and yammered away. Jay was playing chef. Taylor was right by his side. Another scene of people hitting on people. Was there a point to it? I set the salad bowls down. Cindy and Clark were stocking the wash tub with beer, soda and wine. Clink-splash it all went down under the ice filled water. Dan was there. A tiny scar under his chin. A remnant from that party on Menlo Street. He and Jill were speaking again. On again, off again. I think that he's her great love and she his. I went over to Jay and gave him a birthday kiss.

"You and Taylor . . . aren't . . . you know," he said.

"No," I said. He smiled. "What? Now that he's eighteen, you're interested?"

"I didn't mean it like that," he said.

"Yeah, you did," I said and left.

Taylor was talking to one of his new friends. He introduced Andrea to me. A plain girl with a big smile. A little plump. Short, short white hair and wearing a stiff, triangular shaped yellow dress that made her look like a child's rendition of a Christmas tree. I shook her pudgy, little hand and flashed a toothy "hello."

"Hi ya," she said. "Taylor talks lots about you."

"And about you, too," I lied. She positively beamed. Taylor flushed. Another girl called her away. She said she'd be right back.

"She's really nice," he said.

"Seems so. So, how're you doing today?"

"Your friend Jay's horny. He asked me to fuck him."

"He's perpetually horny," I said. "Fuck him if you want to."

Taylor shook his head. "Naww . . . All he talks about is sex." His fingers toyed with the buttons on my shirt. He looked about absently. "I've been wondering . . .," he began as he stared at my chest then pressed his palms flat over my nipples.

"What?"

"Never mind," he said.

"What?"

He patted my chest. "It's my birthday."

"Happy birthday, Taylor."

His fingers felt the matchbook in my pocket. "You're still hung up on that guy, hun . . ."

"Is he here?" I said. "No. Have I seen him? No. Has he

called? No."

"That's not what I asked."

"Ah, Taylor . . . I don't know what the fuck I'm doing. Do you?"

"Know what you're doing? Or what I'm doing?"

"Come on everyone!" Jay's voice sang through the air. Grub was on. The feed bag. Grab a plate and pork. Taylor and I melded into the haphazard line before the grill. Jay plopped burgers onto buns and steaks onto plates. Some vegetarian queen bitched about not finding enough to eat. The potato salad had mayonnaise in it. Mayonnaise has eggs in it. He couldn't eat eggs. The chips, he said, were probably fried in animal lard and how could we all be so gross as to eat this crap. Jill told him shut up or leave. He left.

I sat between Taylor and Jay at one of the two tables that had been set up. Jill, Sue and Steven sat with us. The others scattered themselves across the yard. Connie's stereo blasted a Blondie tune out from within the house.

"We're taking Steve to see Rocky Horror tonight at the Tiffany," said Sue. "Want to come?" Jay emphatically did.

"Sue's afraid to be alone with just me and Jill," Steven said. "We could triple date."

Maul showed up with her vacuum cleaner nose. Her pink tongue magically swallowed Sue's steak. "Hey!!!" Sue cried. Maul pushed between Sue and the table and snorted all over Steven's burger. He quickly gave it up. Sue tried to push the huge beast aside.

"Never argue with an animal who's as big as you are," Steven said.

"Bad girl!" Sue reprimanded her charge. Maul backed shyly away, her head hung low. She flashed us her brown eye. The big, sad eye. Whenever she was in trouble or feeling hurt, she turned her head and stared at you with her big, sad brown eye, until you gave in. Then she'd perk up and cock her bright blue eye at you, put on her doggy grin and beg of you to play. I wished I had that power in my eyes. But I didn't. No one I knew did. God saved that advantage for the animals.

"She looks so sad," Jill said. "Poor baby. C'mere Maul!"

44

Jill held out her burger. Ears piqued, tail wagging, tongue hanging. Maul bounded over and swallowed the burger whole.

"No more," Sue said to the dane. "You'll get sick." Maul, satisfied with her victory, went over to lay in the shade. "Sorry about that," Sue said to us.

"No big deal," said Steven. "Should've given her a steak of her own in the first place. So," he continued," what about tonight? We could make it a triple date?"

"I wouldn't go that far," I said.

"Why not?" asked Jay. "Steve and Jill, me and Taylor, you and Sue. It'll be a lot of fun!"

"Can't go," said Taylor.

"Why not?" Jay asked.

"Just can't."

"But . . ."

"I can't!" Taylor said. Jay's face melted with disappointment.

"Come help me with the cake," Jill said to Jay. "You guys clear the table."

They went inside. Steven carried over a trash can. Sue and I scooped up the garbage and dumped it.

"So, what're you really doing tonight, Taylor?" asked Steven.

"Just kind of wanted a quiet night," he said.

"Are you and he . . ." Sue whispered to me, ". . . going out?"

"His plans are his plans," I said. Does anyone really ever know what's going on? No. Life is to played by ear, I thought. Taylor surprised me by coming over and hugging me. "What's that for?" I said.

"No reason," he said then went over to talk with Andrea.

The bar-b-que wound down around seven. Although most people had a bit too much to drink, not a one was shit faced. Most complained of feeling like a pregnant mare. Everyone dispersed. Jill packed up a piece of left over cake and gave it to Taylor. Kiss-kiss. Goodbye. Taylor and I climbed into my Maverick. Sue, Steven, Jill and Jay piled into Steven's Olds and we went off in separate directions.

When we arrived home, Taylor put his cake into the refrigerator, then disappeared into his room. I crawled into the shower. That was my favourite place to think. Here I was, young, with another summer just beginning. Two more years of college left. The prime of life and I hated it. I was in love with a man I couldn't have - you - and had a man in love with me whom I really didn't think I loved - Taylor.

I heard the bathroom door open. Heard Taylor urinate into the toilet. Heard him flush it. Heard him brush his teeth.

"Do you want the shower?" I asked.

He drew the plastic curtain back, stepped out of his shorts and into the tub. I handed him the soap then stepped out to dry off. This scene wasn't normal to me. Not for two roommates. Kurt and I always waited for the other to be completely finished. I hurriedly wrapped the towel about my waist, gathered up my clothes and went into my room. I was nervous. Didn't know why, exactly, but I was. I fished the matchbook out of my shirt pocket and stared at your phone number. The phone was near me. I'd had a second line hooked up. A separation. From what? You? Taylor? What was I afraid of? The obvious. Intimacy. I could have sex with anyone and just about did. I realized, then, that I, my friends, everyone I even remotely knew, shared that problem. We could fuck anyone, hang out with anyone, but we didn't understand intimacy. Sex was different. It didn't have to last longer than the event itself. Conversation was kept at a minimum. Nobody taught intimacy.

I got dressed. Dressed to stay in. Taylor enveloped himself in a sheath of new clothes. Conservative clothes. I sat on the bed, openly studying him.

"Andrea's asked me to move in with her," he said.

"And?"

"I think I should."

I stretched out over the bedclothes. Was this his way of testing me to see if I was in love with him? I removed a partially smoked cigarette from the night stand ashtray. Straightened it. Lit it. A bitter taste. "When?" I asked.

"Soon." He stared at me, waiting for a reaction. I got up,

slid into my coat and headed out the door.

✳ ✳ ✳ ✳ ✳

I picked up a passenger on my way to the beach. A nun in a bottle. Blue Nun. Spiritual solace and nourishment. I found a blank spot along the coastline. People were gone, cars were gone, just sand and surf and me with the nun.

I sat on the sand and consumed her. All the while waiting for the sea to swallow me like a pill. The tide moved in closer as the greens, browns, reflecting blues and golds of the ocean ran black. The colour of an abyss in the mind. She, the sea, wanted to talk to me. To wrap me in her wet velvet arms.

I watched the water lap at my feet, then gush around me. Her withdrawal was as quick as a brush with a stranger on a crowded sidewalk. She kept coming back. Each caress covering me more completely. Water filled my ears. I could hear the sea pounding, my heart beating. I was being swallowed whole.

Hard hands abruptly yanked me back. Away from the sea. An older man. A vagabond. His face as cracked as a desert basin. His eyes a starburst blue.

"Git offa my beach!" He dragged me farther back to the cool soft sand. "Out!" he yelled. "Git off with ya!" His lower lip split. Its chapped cracks cracking again. His spit ran vermillion.

I sat up and rolled away from him. He kicked me. Hard. In the ass. The Blue Nun made a splashy second showing all over the beach. He kicked me again.

"Git!"

I got. I stumbled back to my car. It was frosted over with a wet cloud. I hunkered over my steering wheel. Wet and dirty, I sat there until dawn.

✳ ✳ ✳ ✳ ✳

After emptying my pockets, I stepped into the shower fully dressed. Warm water washed the sand from my clothes, from my mouth, down the drain. I stripped slowly, slopping soggy material into a pile on the floor. Taylor

47

hadn't been there to greet me. Not that it mattered. I didn't want to see him.

Once I'd cleaned myself, I dumped soap into the filled tub and treaded across the clothes, much in the manner of old wine pressers. All I could think of was clean. Just clean. Wash away the old. Wash away what I'd tried to do.

I hung the garments out to dry, out in what was laughingly called the backyard. A splotch of dirt and choking weeds fenced in by termite ridden wood. Two lengths of rubber coated cording hammered into the side of the house and a nearby tree served as a clothesline. I went back up the rear stairs and went into my room. Taylor had cleaned out my ashtray and cleaned up my room at some point in the night. Your matchbook marked number sat tented in the ashtray. A neat display. Next to it was a note – MAKE THE CALL. You knew where I lived. You knew how to find me. Why should I call? Why should Taylor want me to make the call? Sleep. Sleep called. I answered.

✳ ✳ ✳ ✳ ✳

The telephone jarred me awake. Not totally awake, but enough so to be unable to disregard the incessant ringing. I picked up the receiver and immediately hung it back up. A moment later it was ringing again.

"What?!" I snapped.

"Where the fuck have you been?" It was Jill. "Taylor said you disappeared last night!"

"Took a drive! Okay?"

"No, it's not okay!," she said. "We've been calling around all night!"

"Can't I have time to myself without everyone getting all over my case?"

"I'm coming over!" She hung up on me. I had a choice. Leave, or hash it out with Jill. Leaving would only prolong the confrontation.

I expected her to show up in battle gear. She dressed soft. Not softly, but soft. She radiated with the glow of a seraph. She planned it this way, I was sure. We took our positions. Me on the sofa. She on the love seat. I gave her a

48

bottle of beer, hoping it would help her slip back into insanity. She took a sip then stared. Her stare. Waiting for me to speak. The television clock ticked. I hated anxious silence.

"I went to the beach," I said.

"The beach is closed after sunset."

"Me and an old man. The beach is his after dark."

"So," she said, "what did you see in the dark?"

"A hole."

"Or an asshole?"

"I don't really know," I said.

"Taylor's in love with you."

"I know that."

"I know that you know."

"What am I supposed to do about it?" I asked as I chewed my lip.

"What is it you want?"

My body slumped. Elbows to knees. A view of the floor. "If I knew, you wouldn't be here. I wouldn't be here."

"Do you love Taylor?"

"In a way."

"Do you love Rex?"

"In a way. I think."

"Shouldn't you find out?" She set her bottle down on the coffee table. "I've got to get going. Steven and I are going down to Newport for a week."

"Balboa," I corrected.

"Yeah," she said. "He wants to meet my parents."

Images of pastel bridesmaids flashed in my head. Balboa Island, an open mouth into the sea. She was going to be swallowed whole. "I hope he likes them."

"Yeah," she smiled.

I escorted her out to Sue's car. It was the cavalier thing to do.

"You know," she said, "if you don't find out you may be regretting it forever."

I nodded. She smiled. We kissed. She drove off. I felt lost. Foolish and lost. No one need know about the last aspect. I was used to being my own private fool.

Back in my room, the matchbook glared at me. I picked

up the phone and dialled the number. It rang once, then twice, then . . .

"Hello?"

✳ ✳ ✳ ✳ ✳

You met me at Irv's. A little burger stand on Santa Monica Boulevard. My stomach was experiencing nuclear fusion. Your stomach obviously wasn't. You'd consumed a double burger and a soda, keeping your mouth full at all possible times. I couldn't smell your apple scent. You wore cologne. You looked good, though. Too good. Our silence unnerved me. We'd only said "Hi." You'd already been there waiting. There armed with food to keep your mouth busy.

When you swallowed the last bite and wiped your mouth, you sat back and looked at me, the way a storyteller looks at children.

"Could it work?" you asked.

My reaction must have been odd because you chuckled and broke out in a great smile.

"What is it you expect from me?" I asked.

"I didn't ask you to fall in love. Did I?"

I flushed. My face ran redder than a fire truck. I watched my feet pull away from me as I rose from my seat. Walking over burning coals and shredded glass would have been less painful. Hands in my pocket, I walked away. My eyes glued to the moving pavement. My ears hearing nothing.

Automobile brakes squealed loudly. A horn blared. I'd stepped off the curb, against the light, almost becoming a new hood ornament for a Mercedes. I stood, like a moron, staring at the car, not hearing the driver's obscenities being hurled at me. Your arm yanked me back to the curb. I wouldn't, couldn't look at you. I pulled away and walked back towards Irv's.

"Could it work?!" you said again.

Could it? I didn't know. I'd no experience making "it" work. Taylor's face popped into my mind. His bruised face that day he moved into my life. Zap. It was gone. I stopped. I felt you behind me.

"I don't know," I said. "You came to me. I didn't come to

50

you."

"What if I'm not real?"

I turned around. Looked you in the eye. "You," I said, "are real! Damn you!" I slapped an opened palm against your chest. "There! Real! Others have seen you! You're not a figment of my imagination!"

My hand stayed on your chest. You looked at it, then looked away. I removed my touch. This time you made the motion to leave. Slowly. Walking past me along the sidewalk. You'd just gone after me. Now I went after you. I didn't reach out to stop you, though. Instead, I kept my pace with yours.

"Won't you at least show me where you live?" I asked. "Or is there a reason you won't?"

You stopped. I wasn't sure if it was a sneer or a grin that marked your face. "I can't," you said.

"I'm not good enough?"

"I can't show you where I live right now."

We were at your pick-up truck. You leaned against the side wall, arms loosely crossed in front of your chest.

"This isn't right, Rex!"

"Maybe not."

"What do you want? Guessing games? I'm shit at guessing games!"

"Look," you said. "Will you be home tonight? At seven?"

"No. I have to work until midnight."

"Midnight then?"

It was a question without a response. You walked around to the driver's side of the truck and climbed in. The engine started and you were off. Again. Always again. Leaving me standing on the street.

✳ ✳ ✳ ✳ ✳

Clock watchers make idle workers. I wasn't very good that night. It was slow at the restaurant. A ticky ticked off manager made us all clean. All because he was in a piss poor mood. Spit polish and shine. Windows, brass, wood. He wanted it all gleaming. Taylor had come back that afternoon, while I'd been with you. He cleared out of our place. I had cleared out Kurt for him. Now he cleared himself out from me. What had been the beginning of a promising summer was already dead. As dead as the restaurant was that night. A night when I'd hoped to keep my mind busy.

Midnight came. Became one am. Became one-thirty. I ran a tub full of hot water to soak in. Steam rose. Rivulets of perspiration ran from my scalp, soaking my hair. Cleansing my skin. Clearing my mind of all thought. All that mattered was slipping off. Into real sleep. Drip, drip, drip. The faucet spoke. Loudly. I could feel my heart beating. The executioner's drum beat within. The din assaulting the grey matter in my head. My temples pounded. The sound was suffocating. An anxious asthmatic gasp. My hand slid to my chest. I felt my heart pounding. It slid down to my stomach, then crotch, then thigh, feeling this form of mine as a blind man might.

There were footsteps in the kitchen. Cautious steps. I stilled myself in the water. The footsteps came closer then stopped before the bathroom door.

The door flew open as if a cyclone had struck. Its old centre panel split like a cow's skull at a slaughterhouse. Splinters of the door jamb sprayed through the room. He lunged for me. I sank under the water under his falling weight. I heard his skull crack against the tile. My hand found the spigot. I yanked myself up from under him. He grabbed me and tried to pull me back down as he tried to regain his balance. I fell back on him, knocking his head against the handles of the faucet. My elbow knocked his head back under the water. I didn't see his hand though. I never saw the blade of his knife as it grazed my side. I jumped, then fell out of the tub, the blood spreading like a wild fire across my wet skin. He tried to get up again. As I stepped back a large splinter of wood jabbed into my foot. No thoughts. Just reaction. The deodorant must've blinded his eyes for his scream implied I'd gouged them out.

*****

52

"I'm so sorry," Taylor said. "Fahad knows a lot of people. He must've tracked me down."

"Must've," I said. The paramedics had cleaned the wound. A couple of butterfly bandages. The cut burned as steadily as a candle. The blood still seeping out. "I told the police that I didn't know him."

"I told them," he said, "that he was after me. You've got to file a complaint."

"Shit."

"He'll be out and he'll be back."

"By the next time," I said, "I'll have your new address and phone number tattooed on my chest."

Taylor sighed. A resolved sigh. "I didn't mean for this to happen."

"I know."

"Can I . . .?"

"I don't need your help."

"Can I do anything for you?"

"I want to hate you right now. You know that, don't you."

"Yeah."

"But I can't. And it pisses me off to no end that I can't."

He helped me back to my room, then mopped up the mess in the bathroom. He found some old Sleep-Eze in my nightstand drawer. I took them. That heavy rum-dumb sleep hit.

*****

I could feel myself sweating. Sticky eyes opened in response. Dirty heat beat through those brown rinsed blinds next to my bead. My side throbbed. My head even worse.

"Want some aspirin?"

I turned towards the voice. Your voice. You were there low on the floor, your back upright, supported by bolster pillows between you and the wall.

"I want a cigarette," I said. My mouth was as dry as the ocean was wet. You stood up, lit a cigarette for me then placed it between my lips. An ashtray came to rest by my hand.

"Taylor called me."

I remembered the matchbook. He went out of bounds, I thought. Way out of bounds calling you.

"He and Jill," you continued, "are getting the bathroom door replaced. She said the scene shop at the school had spares."

"So now I can't even take a piss in private." My bricks started caving in. A rumble as loud as an earthquake. Maybe I was just hungry. Taylor called you. You came. A great many dialogues ran through my brain.

"Should we call your parents?"

"I'll call them later. The less they have to worry about the better."

You sat on the bed, next to me, and pulled back the bedclothes down to my waist. The bandage registered the night's letting - now clotted blobs of brown-red. I pulled the sheet back up over the wound. You smiled a soft smile and left the room.

I'm not a crier by nature, but my eyes filled to overflowing with salty tears. My wall caved in completely. I was hungry. But not for food. Nothing's worse than having a taste for something that nothing satiates. Ring. The front door bell rang. Not a pleasant ring, more like a fire alarm. I heard your weight descending the stairs to answer. Ring again. Thud, clomp. The door shut. Thud, clomp, thud, clomp up the stairs. Silence. A laugh. Soon, Sue was in my room. She tossed me a bag of Nestle Crunch bars and some roses.

"Hi," she said. "The Crunch bars are from Maul. She said to save her a couple of bites. The roses are from me."

"Give Maul a kiss from me. Right on her runny, cold snout."

"Sore?"

"Some. It looks worse than it is."

You entered again with a bowl of water, a washcloth, peroxide and fresh bandages atop a TV tray. Sue moved to the foot of my bed to make room for you.

"I presume the two of you met on the stairs," I said.

"Yeah," Sue said. She sat in silence watching as you

54

swabbed then redressed the wound for me. When finished, you packed up your supplies and left the room.

"He's handsome," she said.

"Very. But about as reliable as diarrhoea."

"Taylor's very nice, too. I guess I can see your problem."

"And what does Jill have to say about it?"

Sue shifted uneasily. "She understands. But you already know that. Maybe you should think hard about what it is that you want. Taylor's young, but he's an old soul. You know all about him. He knows about himself. He's honest. Rex, though, you know what you know."

"I don't think I could deal with anymore surprises like Fahad."

"Yeah," she sighed. "What do I know? I'm a biology major."

You came in again. Sue smiled at me, said her good-bye and left. You stood leaning against the wall for the longest time, staring at me. A blank stare. I didn't want to see what you were seeing, so I stared back. The sun had made your skin a little more buttery brown, brought out a few more freckles on your cheeks and nose. Your pale brown hair was bleaching to a faded wheat. I felt like an old, salted piece of dried cod by comparison.

"She thinks," you said, "that you should choose Taylor."

"The choice isn't mine alone."

"No?"

"No."

You nodded absently then moved to the desk chair. Again you stared. At the three paper spheres that hung from the corner of the ceiling. Old party decorations. One navy, one white, one pale blue to commemorate a party I'd long since forgotten.

"Which one do you like least?" you asked as you pointed to the spheres.

"The pale blue."

"That's you," you said. "I'm the dark blue. Taylor's the white. Which one to you like best?"

"Both," I said. "And I don't like the analogy."

"I don't like making choices," you said. "I can't. If I say

yes and it doesn't work out, where would that leave us?"

"At about the same place we're at now."

"So, I say no and you and Taylor become one. Does that make you happy?"

"Taylor's wants are as unsure as my own."

"Then maybe we should let it rest while we let you rest."

You came back to the bed, handed me the glass of water, now warm and stale, then shook out some triangular shaped, pale yellow pills from a prescription bottle and handed those to me as well.

"What're those?"

"Some pills I had. They'll help you sleep."

I took the pills. They hung up for a moment in my dry mouth before the wave of water sent them packing into my acidic, knotted stomach. You set the glass aside then sat back down at the desk and waited for me to fall asleep.

❋ ❋ ❋ ❋ ❋

I slept the sleep of the dead. I dreamed their dreams. Nothing. Coming to was like awakening in a drunken haze. Those three spheres hanging in the corner of the ceiling became my focal point. Three bodies suspended. Going nowhere.

You were gone. Everyone was gone. I got up and walked through the house unaware of my nudity. Just looking for someone - anyone. My stomach rumbled. There wasn't so much as a can of tuna left in the cupboards. The hunger pangs. Then it happened. Those pangs were quelled by my mason's trowel. It worked overtime replacing the bricks. Trowel mortar bricks. The pattern. Faster and faster. Reinforced this time. A double wall to protect myself from the double curse of you and Taylor.

❋ ❋ ❋ ❋ ❋

The reflection that faced me in the mirror was a stranger. Matted hair, dark crescents underlining my sunken eyes. My lower lip was split-scabbed over. Greasy growth of whiskers bruised my face.

I wanted to lock myself in the bathroom, but there was

56

no door. No. Jill had had it removed. I didn't want to deal with the court ordeal of Fahad. I didn't want to deal with anything. I popped some aspirin, then crawled into the shower. My sanctuary. I washed and shaved as carefully as possible, but the wound's dressing came undressed. There was no way to wash my entire body, short of wrapping myself in Handi-Wrap, that would avoid the wound. It bled a little. The soap stung. I thought about rubbing salt in the cut. I'd heard that salt would make a cut scar hellaciously. I could tell all sorts of terrible tales about how it had come to be. The soap, though, stung enough to knock the sense back into my head.

I dressed the slice as neatly as I could. I felt almost new again. A new face, new bricks and a new resolve. Fuck falling in love. Feeling dead felt better. Go and crawl back into my own dark place.

My co-workers at the restaurant were surprised to see me. My manager had been notified of my attack by someone unnamed but someone I suspected. The rest of the waitstaff had already divided up my shifts. Most were less than pleased to give them back. Cut throats.

It was busy that night and I moved slowly. A bit of blood leaked through my shirt midway through shift. This did little for the appetites of some diners, but did marvellous much for their sympathetic generosity. I made a fortune in tips.

Jay, Clark and Dina were my last party seated. The hostess stuck them in a far corner booth. They, too, were surprised to see me working.

"What're you trying to prove, you idiot?" Dina said.

"I'm not dead."

"Shit," laughed Jay. "We ordered flowers for you."

Dina flipped open her menu. "So, I guess it doesn't hurt."

"It's just annoying," I said. "You want drinks?"

"That's a joke, right?" said Clark. "You know our routine. Keep'em coming 'til the bar closes up."

I served the trio, then set about finishing up my clean up duty. By 11:30 everything was done. I made them pay up their tab so that the cashier could close up and go home. I then joined them at their table.

"We're going to Studio One," said Jay. "Want to come?"

"He needs to be asleep," said Dina.

"That's all I've done all day," I said as I reached for Jay's glass of wine. Dina slapped my hand.

"Are you nuts?" she barked. "Drink that shit and you'll be bleeding all over the place."

"Geez, Dina! Leave him alone!" Clark said. "That little bit won't kill him."

Dina screwed up her face. "You know," she said, "I've really got to expand my social circle. I'm getting a rep as a fag hag running around with you guys all the time. Dino says I should give you up."

"Who's Dino?" I asked.

"Her new boyfriend," Jay and Clark said in unison. Their laughter was to the point of being cruel. Dina chewed on her lip, then suddenly spat on them.

"Hey!"

"What's the big idea?!" said Jay as he wiped his face.

"You're assholes! Everyone's either a joke or another fuck to you!"

"Jesus Christ! Dino's a dickhead!" said Clark.

"And a Bible thumper to boot!" added Jay.

I turned to Dina. "You're dating a holy roller?"

"He's not!" she said.

"But you're Jewish," I said.

"Only half! And, like I said, he's not a holy roller!"

"Then why's he got all that religious crap?" asked Clark.

"Come on, guys," I said. "Studio One closes in a couple of hours."

"I'm not going," said Dina.

"Suit yourself," said Jay as he and Clark slid out from the booth. They tossed off their good-byes and left. Dina slumped in her seat.

"Why can't they just accept?" she said. "They put down every guy I go out with. It's stupid. Neither of them is interested in me."

"I don't know," I said. "Why don't you go over to Dino's now?"

58

"It's too late. He's usually asleep by ten thirty."

"So? Go and wake him up."

She smiled. "He wouldn't like that."

"Make him like it."

❋ ❋ ❋ ❋ ❋

Dina dropped me off at my house. She decided to take the risk. With a honk and a wave, she was off. I went inside, hoping someone would be there. Wrong. I was still alone. Whenever I'm surrounded by people, I crave privacy. But now was too private. I wanted some comforting body around me. Someone I could nestle with on the couch while an old Bewitched rerun played on the vidiot box. I wanted to be bewitched. And I was. With them. And I didn't want to be.

The cut on my side made it impossible to venture into West Hollywood for a night at the 8709, the best bath house in Los Angeles. I could hang with a variety of kinky types, but not someone into blood. No blood. No shit. I remembered Taylor's trick and the scar on his back.

I washed up a bit then changed the bandage. I soaked the bloodstain on my shirt with hydrogen peroxide. It fizzed the stain out. I left it soaking in the bathroom sink. What else to do? Nothing. Television. Nothing. My own room felt alien. Like a hospital ward. I went into Kurt's, then Taylor's, old room. The bed was nude. I stretched out on the bed. Tried to smell Taylor in the mattress. It just smelled musty. I flattened out, mindful of the wound, and slid into sleep.

❋ ❋ ❋ ❋ ❋

I was painting houses. Houses floating in the air. Strange colours. Pink with brown trim. Aquamarine and orange. Green grass, dotted with yellow spots, rolled over undulating hills way below. Then Lisa came out of the pink house. Lisa, the wonderful girl I'd spoken with often on campus, but never ran around with. She had the most beautiful lapis eyes. They blazed a holy blue. Her severe striking features were softened by a mound of wavy ebony hair. She just smiled and waved at me as I continued to paint. I painted and waved back. She stepped off the porch

59

and glided onto the rolling grass, carried away by the motion.

Some say to dream is to listen to the subconscious, the super conscious. I thought maybe this dream to be divine intervention. Thought God was speaking to me. Did I believe in God? Yes. I did. But that was all and why should God speak to me anyway? I was a heathen. A true heathen slut.

I spent the early part of the morning debating the dream. By nine o'clock, I figured it was just a form of D.T.'s. I washed up in the sink, hung my shirt up to dry, then changed the dressing on my cut. I hadn't been scheduled to work that day, so I was free. Free to make my own time. I ran a list through my mind of people to see and people not to see. I decided that I didn't want to see any of them.

✻ ✻ ✻ ✻ ✻

Across from USC's campus, across Exposition Boulevard, was the rose garden. Though gang members sometimes roosted there, to mug unsuspecting people, I felt it to be safe. Red and yellow roses lined the grass walkways. It was a beautiful spot, save for the occasional frantic bee, to walk and to think. I liked roses. Sue had given me roses. Sue was nice. She didn't deserve the shit Jill and I put her through.

"Fancy finding you here."

I turned. There she was, smiling. Lisa. Lisa in a summer dress. I smiled. She came up beside me and we walked down the garden path.

"Uncanny," I said.

"What?"

"Had a dream about you last night. Well, not about you exactly. It was about painting houses. But you were in it."

"That's nice," she said.

"Why're you here by yourself?" I asked. "It's not all that safe."

"I'm safe."

"You've a guardian angel with a black belt?"

She laughed. "Maybe I do."

I stopped before a bush. The roses were almost red-black.

Goblets of burgundy drinking up the sun.

"Pick one," she said.

"I can't. They're all too beautiful."

"But there must be one. One that you're especially drawn to," she said as she gently cupped a fully exploded bloom between her fingers. "This one's mine. All of its soul exposed to creation. No secrets to hide."

My eye caught sight of a small bud, caught between the crush of a cluster of full blooms. "Here," I said. "Here's my fellow."

"Good," she said. "Now he'll have the strength to burst out into fullness while all the others shy away into rose hips. He may be the last seen, but also the last forgotten."

"You're weird."

"Maybe so," she laughed. "Maybe so, but I don't care."

"I wish I could see things like you do," I said as we continued.

"I'm not always happy, you know. But I'm never as unhappy as you."

"As me?"

"And your friends. "I know many of them."

"I know," I said.

"That's why I don't run with you all."

"Who then do you run with?"

"Myself mostly," she said. "And with whomever I meet that day."

We walked out of the garden, back into reality. The sky seemed dirtier from out street perspective. Dirtier, noisier, hostile even.

"Are you hungry?" she asked. I nodded. "Come on."

We jaywalked across Exposition then went into the Commons on campus. Their summer fare was slim. We chose sandwiches, fruit and drinks and headed out with our cache. Lisa led me not to the main dining room, not to the concrete bird shit spattered picnic tables just outside, but instead made me trek to a secluded little chapel behind the Hancock building. No one was there. Just us and the plants.

"This spot reminds me a bit of New England," she said.

"I'd never noticed it before."

"You're not the only one. No matter how crowded it gets everywhere else, I always find this place deserted."

"So," I said, "why were you in the garden?"

"To walk. To enjoy," she said. "People think I'm a little eccentric."

"You were dating that Sigma guy, weren't you?" She nodded as she bit through the skin of her orange. "Where's he?"

"He went back to Phoenix for the summer. His name's John."

"So, what do you think?" I asked.

"About?"

"Are you going to marry John?"

She laughed. "Oh God no!"

"Why not?"

"Why for?"

"I dunno," I said.

"John's a nice guy, but we have different values. He's 210% WASP. He's got his life planned out well beyond retirement. I can't live that sort of structured life."

"Seems to me," I said, "that it doesn't hurt to have a plan."

"Look," she said as she ripped apart her orange, "his kind of order wouldn't allow for spontaneous walks in the rose garden, wouldn't allow for an impromptu picnic like we're having now. His is a military life. Not for me."

"Makes sense."

"If you enjoy living," she said, "then order only works for those who are afraid to live."

"You don't get rich riding with Chaos, though," I said.

"Is that what you want? To be rich?"

"I know, I know. They say that money can't buy happiness, but it could make misery taste a whole lot better."

She pointed an orange filled hand at me. "You're bleeding."

"Shit."

I unbuttoned my shirt and pulled it back away from the wound.

"Say red rose three times," she said. I felt stupid but I did what she said. She then took her palm, licked the orange from it and pressed it on top of the bandage. Strange. The pressure didn't hurt. It tingled a bit. She withdrew her hand. "There," she said. "It won't bleed anymore."

I buttoned up my shirt. "Is that voodoo?"

"Maybe," she said. "Maybe it's just rose red."

"Blood can fertilize the roses."

"So, what's up with you this summer?"

"Work," I said. "I should get a full time job, but I'd have to give it up come fall."

"Seems to me that you don't really want to be rich."

"I'm lazy."

"Lazy's okay. You just haven't figured out what you want out of life."

"What is it that you want?"

"To be . . . a part of everything and then some."

"That's not very precise," I said.

"Not in your mind."

"But it is in yours?" I said as I bit into my apple. The right kind of apple. Crisp. Tart white meat. Juicy. And very, very scented. I remembered you all of a sudden. How did you come by your apple scent?

"Yes," she said.

"I wish I could understand it."

"Got anything to do today?"

"No. Just hanging around."

"Come by my place."

I agreed. We picked up our litter and dropped it in the trash. Lisa washed the sticky orange from her hand at a water fountain. She shook them out to dry.

"Here," I said. "Wipe them on my jeans."

She laughed, crouched down and did just that. Used my pant leg for a towel. As we walked across the campus, then down to 27th Street via Hoover Avenue, she listened to my idle babble about you and Taylor. Never once did she seem to feign interest.

* * * * *

63

Her apartment suited her. A nice large studio space in a clean stucco building. Gray carpeting. White white walls. A corner unit with windows on two sides. She said she chose this one because it faced east. She liked the feel of the early morning sun. Her double bed and nightstand took up one corner of the room. A wall unit, made from sturdy baker's shelves, held a small television set, a stereo and baskets. Baskets filled with girlish stuff. Small stuffed animals, colognes, lacy looking things and make-up.

I sat in one of her two overstuffed chairs. A rather large round table, high enough to serve as a desk, was somewhat between the two chairs. She brought us some iced tea, then sat in the other chair.

"Well," she said.

"I like this place. I've a two bedroom over on 32nd."

"I know where you live. We've walked home together before."

"But I was always the first stop."

"True," she said. "So, this Taylor's moved out?"

"Yeah."

"And Rex has disappeared?"

"That's the sum of it."

"It's simple to see. You like being needed and wanted, yet at the same time, you despise it. Taylor needs, or needed, too much. Rex doesn't really need at all."

I hated hearing what I already knew about myself but refused to admit. I wanted her to give me permission to say 'Fuck them both.' She didn't say that.

"I think," she said, "you should just let them run their own courses. Try some prayer and meditation to let the confusion go."

"Maybe I should just write them both off."

"But you don't want to. You can't control anyone's actions but your own. And only you can control your reactions. Too many people our age are walking around like shellacked zombies without any sense of love for themselves."

"Yeah yeah, how can you love someone else if you can't love yourself blah blah blah."

"You're afraid that it's true. You don't like that, do you," she said softly.

"It's hard. They don't give you an operator's manual when you come out of the womb."

"Your manual is in here," she said, pressing her palm against her breast. "You've just got to learn how to read it."

"Again, no manual."

"Okay," she said. "That's fair. But you should learn where to look for answers."

"Self-help books?"

"Perhaps. Maybe something broader."

"Look, Lisa, I'm a bit dense. You can spell it out for me."

"Okay, a simple task. Every morning and every evening, say, 'I release all forms of negativity from my mind and body . . .'"

"That's it?"

"If you don't believe what you say, then say it a hundred or a thousand times daily until you do."

"Now you're getting complicated. I'm lazy, remember?"

"Yes, I do," she said. She leaned in towards me. "Because you have fear." The telephone rang before she could go on. She excused herself to answer it. I made up my excuse to leave. I got up and took my glass to the sink. She interrupted her call. "Don't go yet . . ."

"I have to."

"You said you had nothing to do."

"Today," I said, "But I'm going out with friends this evening." I kissed her cheek. "Thank you."

She told her caller to hang on a minute. She scratched her number on a piece of paper towelling and handed it to me. "Call if you've a need to."

"Thanks again," I said as I left. She struck a nerve, she did. My whole nervous system. She was right. I did have fear. Of everything. It had been a pleasant day up until then. The rose garden, the picnic . . . .. My wound. It didn't throb, didn't itch, didn't anything. I felt the bandage through my shirt. It was still there. I'd check it once I got home.

The house was still there. The sight of it made me aware of the fact that I either had to get a new roommate, or move out. One of the advantages of a month to month tenancy is being able, almost, to just pick up and move. I had to make a decision. I decided to take a nap.

My room felt a little less foreign to me as I tossed my shirt onto the floor, then pulled the bandage off. The cut, which that morning had been a bruised, scabby mess, was sealed. A pinkish line with only a hint of brown bruising showing. Either I was like a quick healing cat, or Lisa was a healer. Maybe she did have something to teach me.

Jill called that night from Newport. She and Steven were fine and how was I. I hadn't seen her since she left. When she and Steven stopped by to see me the morning after my knifing, I was still out of it. It was she and Steven, not she and Taylor as you had said, who took my bathroom door to be replaced. Taylor was supposed to have called Jay and Clark to pick up the new one from the scene shop. I told Jill that I hadn't seen or heard from Taylor since that day. She said they were staying with her parents another two weeks, but she would call Jay and Clark for me and tell them to go get the door. I said thanks and we let it go at that.

*****

My ad for a roommate ran in the paper for two weeks. In that time I had only four responses. Two men who couldn't speak much English, a soon-to-be Freshman jock named Eddie who didn't want to live in the dorms, and a devoutly feminist Graduate student.

Also in those two weeks, I found out that the police had enough on Fahad to deport him. So, going against everyone's better judgement, I declined to file a complaint. A complaint meant a trial and a trial meant my "character" being assaulted on the stand. Forget it. Let them ship him back to Iraq or wherever he came from.

As to the prospective roomies, I couldn't deal with a language barrier, so Jae-Suk from Korea and Javier from Costa Rica went bye-bye. Gloria, the feminist Graduate student was in the running until she told me that she didn't mind if I smoked, so long as I did it in my room only. Sorry, Gloria. That left the Frosh jock, Eddie. I told him that I was gay. He said he didn't care. I said that he would have shit to pay if his team mates found out he was living with a reputed fag. He said he didn't care. I said I had guests coming in and out of all of the time. He said that he didn't care. Fine. I called Mrs. Austin, the landlady, and sent his application on to her. Like Eddie, she didn't care. Just pay the rent on time.

✽ ✽ ✽ ✽ ✽

"He's a ball player?" Jill asked, not believing.

"Seems odd, don't you think?" I asked.

"Very."

"But I need to pay the rent."

"Well, I hope it works out," she said. "How's the scar?"

I lifted up my shirt to show her. The brown was gone. Only a pink line remained. She gingerly touched it. My stomach muscles quivered. Eddie, chomping on an apple, came in from the kitchen.

"Neat scar," he said. "How'd ya get it?"

"A man tried to kill me in the bathtub," I said.

"Where'd it happen?"

"Here," I said. I thought he was going to choke on his apple.

"Fuck!" he said.

"That's what I said, I think."

Jill laughed. Eddie continued chewing on his apple. "Shit man," he said. "Any fuckers come at me in here are gonna get their dentures knocked into next Tuesday." He turned on the television and parked himself on the couch. Jill kissed me good-bye, then threw Eddie a teasing wink before she left. Eddie got up and changed the channel. Changed it again. And again. None of the programs interested him. He shut it off. "She's pretty," he said.

"She's taken," I said.

"How come all you kind of guys know pretty chicks?"

"Because we're not interested in their crotches," I said.

"Seems like a good gimmick to get'em, ya know?"

"You'd have to put on too good of a show," I said.

"How d'ya mean?"

"They'll expect to see you occasionally making out with

67

a guy."

"Oh . . ." he said, then, "You mind if I bring, ya know, a chick by?"

"What? Overnight?"

"Yeah."

"It's your bedroom. I screw in my room. You screw in your room. The living room and kitchen are out of bounds."

"Cool," he said. "So, you got an ol' man?"

"Not at the moment."

"Me neither," he said, not realizing what'd he'd said. I got it.

The doorbell rang. I answered it. Lisa was there, bearing red, red roses. She brought them as a sort of housewarming gesture, to welcome my new roommate. Eddie drooled at the sight of her. She kissed him hello. I was sure he creamed his jeans. Lisa didn't stay long. She invited me to attend a lecture that night. I accepted. She said she'd pick me up at seven, then left.

"God!" Eddie panted. "She's a fuckin' babe! I can't stand it . . ."

"When was the last time you got laid?"

He blushed and stammered something about last Christmas. I laughed. He got flustered. "It's been awhile! Okay?!" he said as he crammed the last of his apple into his mouth.

"Are you a virgin?"

"No!"

"Fine," I said. "But please don't tie up the bathroom until you get laid again."

I went into my room to lay out what I'd wear that evening. A lecture, she said. I didn't ask the topic. Dress neutral. Dress preppie. Maybe after the lecture we could hop on over to the Odessy. I hadn't been there in ages.

✳ ✳ ✳ ✳ ✳

Lisa's Cutlass was old, but clean. And it ran beautifully. She manoeuvred through the unusually dense freeway traffic with ease.

"He's cute," she said.

68

"Cute, yes, but I'm beginning to think I made a mistake. He's a breeder."

"A what?"

"A breeder. Straight. Hetero. Macho," I said.

"And that's bad?"

"Not bad. Just problematic. A young, straight jock living with me, for God's sake? It isn't normal."

"Maybe he's not so straight," she said.

"He is. Where are we going anyhow?

"To Santa Monica."

"What's the lecture on?"

"New Age stuff."

"What's that?"

"The New Age. It's coming."

Somewhere in my mind, the circuits flashed back to my first encounter with Taylor at Venice Beach. He'd babbled something about Neptune or Pluto or one of those mythological gods. I had been a little too wasted to remember.

I was never very good at finding my way in Santa Monica or Venice Beach. I usually just aimed the old Maverick at the ocean and parked thereabouts, making short lived mental notes of the routes I walked. At night my sense of direction in alien areas defected completely. Lisa, though, seemed to know this area intimately. She led us to a large bland building. We entered through a side door and went up a small flight of stairs.

The room, the lecture room, was either too small or just appeared small due to the many, many folding chairs crowded within. A woman with an Earth Mother persona ladled out fruit juice into paper cups. Those waxy kind of cups that leaked. We took some juice and sat towards the back of the room. People kept filing into the room for the next fifteen or so minutes. Some said hi to Lisa. She returned every greeting with a smile.

"Is this anything like EST?" I asked.

"No. Just relax."

"I am. Confidentially, I tried your prayers, or whatever they are. I think they've helped. At least I'm not downing

69

the Nun at the beach anymore."

She laughed as if she understood my closing statement. That was her only unnerving quality. She always knew. I suspected her to be psychic, but never asked. A tuning fork hummed. I looked up. Another Earth Mother type was at the dais.

"Welcome," she said. "All are welcome. Our special guest this evening is Mr. Carl Suffolk." Everyone clapped. "He'll be speaking on the topic of our rebirth in this modern age."

Mr. Suffolk, an average size man of about forty-five, with eyes and hair the colour of Lisa's, stood up and smiled as he approached the dais. He radiated warmth and good will.

"Thank you," he said. "Cayce spoke to us of Atlantis. Of Lemuria. Of the five senses of man. Tonight we'll discuss these topics and the reincarnation of the 25,000, the seeded people and their helpers, whose task is to evoke the awakening in our fellow men and women."

I heard the door creak open. Mr. Suffolk smiled, acknowledging the late comer. I turned to see him or her. It was a him. It was you. You sat shyly in a chair near the door. Mr. Suffolk continued his talk. My ears went blind. My eyes went deaf. I couldn't see what he spoke of, nor hear what I saw. Just you. For all the changes the last few weeks had brought me, you still had the power to hammer at my bricks. Time seemed to stop for me.

"You asleep?" Lisa prodded.

"No," I said. "Just lost in thought."

"It's a break."

I looked at your chair. You weren't there. Lisa told me where the bathroom was. We had twenty minutes. I got up and left the room. I needed to smoke. No smoking allowed in the room. I went just outside the building and sat on the steps.

I puffed and puffed, trying to cloud my thoughts with smoke. I didn't want to see you, but hoped I'd run into you. Mr. Carl Suffolk stepped out of the building, taking a cleansing breath of wet night air.

"Hello," he said when he spotted me.

"Hi," I said, feeling like a kid caught smoking in the boys room at school.

"I don't recall seeing you here before," he said as he sat on the step, next to me. I took one last drag off the cigarette then killed it.

"A friend brought me," I said.

"Who?"

"Lisa."

"Lisa with the incredible blue eyes?" he said. I looked at him strangely. He smiled. "Lisa Kanton," he said. I nodded. "She's my niece."

"She didn't tell me you were her uncle."

"Well, it's kind of like we're all family," he said. He had such charisma. As much, maybe more, as you.

One of the Earth Mothers came out and beckoned Mr. Suffolk to return. We helped each other up and went back into the room. Lisa was talking with you. I went straight to my seat. Everyone sat back down as soon as Mr. Suffolk returned to the dais. The lecture continued for another forty minutes. It was a little past ten when it ended.

Lisa whispered to me, "You've already met my uncle, haven't you?"

"Why didn't you tell me?"

We got up and moved toward the dais, but the crush of people fawning over Mr. Suffolk immobilized us. I was glad because I didn't know what to say to him. My mind had been on you the entire time.

"You were talking to Rex at the break," I said.

"Who?"

"Rex," I said. "You and he were talking when I came back in."

"Was that the man you're in love with?"

"Can you say it a little louder?"

She laughed. "I'm sorry. He just started talking to me. You know, idle chit chat."

"About?"

"The lecture."

"Lisa!" Carl broke through his adoring crowd and gave Lisa a most earnest hug. "Your Mom said you'd probably

71

be here."

"You knew I wouldn't miss it."

"And you," he turned to me, "the mad smoker."

"Hello, again," I said.

Lisa made the formal introductions. We stayed to help the crew of Earth Mommas and Poppas restore janitorial order to the room. Carl invited us to have dinner with him and his friend.

✳ ✳ ✳ ✳ ✳

"Who's his friend?" I asked as we drove weaving around corners and one-way streets.

"I don't know," she said. "Carl knows everyone it seems. He's an Aquarian like you."

"I don't know everyone."

"No, but it seems like you do," she said.

I left it at that. Let her drive the rest of the way to the restaurant in peace. Whatever it was that gave her that serene quality she had, I wanted. She had the same innate optimism that my doe-eyed ex, Michael, had. I couldn't understand its existence in some people while so many others, such as myself, were constantly splooshing up and down in life's washing machine.

✳ ✳ ✳ ✳ ✳

Carl was already seated in a booth, waiting for us and his other guest. He kissed Lisa hello and had us sit. They made the necessary small talk about the family. I politely listened. A nod. A yes. An "Oh, really?" Chat-chat. I perused the menu. Not a lick of meat to be found. No booze of any sorts. Clean vegetarian all the way. Some might have called it healthy. I set the menu aside. Carl smiled at me.

"You should have the stuffed artichoke," he said.

"What makes you think I like artichokes?" I said.

Carl smiled at me. "You do," he said. He was a very handsome man. Just a few pounds overweight, but that made him more attractive to me. The last thing I needed was to lust after Lisa's uncle.

72

The hostess appeared out of nowhere and handed Carl a note. He read it, thanked her, then stuffed it in his shirt pocket.

"What is it?" Lisa asked.

"It's just going to be the three of us."

"Stood up?" I asked.

"Tell me something," he said. Just then the waitress appeared. I always appreciate a waitron with timing. Carl gave her our order, then turned his attention back to me. "Tell me something," he said again. "Do you enjoy being who you are?"

"I can't be anyone else," I said.

"Then who are you?"

"Come on, Carl," Lisa said. "Don't pick on him."

"But I'm not. Am I?"

I didn't know how to respond. His question wasn't malicious. Wasn't anything more than a direct, honest question. I did understand it. That's what bothered me the most.

"Why do you ask?" I finally said.

"Because there's something about you that I like," he said. "You have to understand that I mean no harm in asking. But, I can sense that something's been troubling you most of the evening."

"My mind wanders," I said.

"Where to?" he asked.

"That, I'm never sure."

"Rex," said Lisa. "You're thinking about Rex" I felt my face flush. I didn't want to discuss this in front of a stranger. Lisa turned to Carl. "He's the guy who came in late to the lecture."

"Nice looking fellow," Carl said.

"He's not one of your disciples?" I asked.

"Never saw him before."

"He was very interested in the subject," said Lisa.

"You told me it was all chit chat."

"It was. About the lecture."

I sighed and slumped back in my seat. "He keeps coming in and out of my life and I think I want him in."

73

"But," said Carl, "he doesn't know what he wants."

"That's it. A very simple equation. One plus one plus uncertainty equals a fraction of one."

"Have you asked him what he's afraid of?" asked Lisa.

"What if it doesn't work out."

"Then at least you've tried," said Carl. "Fear breeds hesitation. Hesitation breeds inaction. Inaction breeds paralysis."

"I still don't understand how," I said. "I can't make him do what he doesn't want to do."

"Exactly," said Carl. "Ergo, you remain active. Doing is better than fretting."

"Besides," said Lisa, "is Taylor completely out of the picture?"

"No. He's still working at the restaurant. We're never scheduled at the same time, though."

"We are what we make ourselves," said Carl.

"Then what is it that you created in yourselves to make you positive types?" I asked.

Lisa and Carl exchanged glances. They were too, too alike in looks and thought. They should have been twins. Lisa looked at me. "We see a purpose in life," she said. "You would've heard Carl's talk on that very matter if you hadn't allowed Rex to close you up."

"It's an automatic reflex. Like picking a scab."

"Then pick it," said Carl. "Go to him and talk. You can find him if you've a mind to."

✸ ✸ ✸ ✸ ✸

Lisa dropped me off around twelve thirty. The house was dark. I could hear Eddie snoring in his room. I had Carl's number in my pocket. He had invited me to visit him if I had a mind to. I think I did.

I scoured my teeth and washed my face, then proceeded into my room, undressing on the way. I shut my door and flicked on the light in the same instance.

"You're new roommate would've done well working in the Spanish Inquisition," Taylor said.

"What're you doing here?"

"I thought I left something behind."

"Eddie let you in?"

He held up his key. "I had a duplicate," he said. "Eddie? Is that his name?" I nodded. "I told him I owed you some money, but I wanted to give it to you in person, so there'd be no misunderstandings."

"Give me the key, please," I said. He set it on the nightstand. "So," I continued, "what's the real reason for this visit?"

"Dunno . . .," he said not looking at me but at the floor.

"I'm working breakfast tomorrow."

"I got another job. Waitering at Julie's."

"Good for you."

"Andrea's in love with me. She says. Keeps after me to fuck her."

"You don't want to?"

"God no!"

"So, just say no," I said.

"I woke up this morning. She was all over me."

"While you were sleeping?"

"She woke me up with her mouth on my crotch."

"What'd you do?"

"Pushed her off. She got mad and started yelling some shit, then started crying. Gross."

"Well," I said, "I'm sorry it's turned into a problem for you."

"I gotta move."

"Do what you have to do," I said. Silence. He stared into space. I finished undressing. "I have to go to sleep, Taylor."

"Oh." He got up from the bed. I climbed into it. He just stood there, lost. "What . . ." he started. Pause. Spit it out, I thought. I hated this dance. Finally, "Could . . . could I crash here tonight?"

"Then what about tomorrow night?" I said. "You've paid rent. You've a right to live there."

"But she's ruined it! Don't you see that?! She's made it impossible for me to stay!"

"You want me to help you fix your problem. Is that it?"

"I just need . . . Oh forget it!" he snapped. "You're too

75

damned wrapped up in yourself!"

"Maybe so," I said. "I didn't invite your ex-pimp here to knife me. Nor did I expect you to bail on me as you did after that! I'm no more wrapped up in myself than you are with your shit!"

I could see Taylor's energy drain from him like a court martialed cadet. His head hung. Hands slid quietly into his pockets. I wanted to say yes, but that would've been unfair to Eddie.

"Where were you tonight?" he asked.

"Out. With Lisa."

"Oh . . ."

"Look," I said. "Can't you call one of your other friends?"

"They're all Andrea's friends. Not mine."

"Fuck it," I said. "Stay the night if you want. I've got to get up in six hours." I rolled over to face the windows. "Turn out the light when you're ready."

✵ ✵ ✵ ✵ ✵

The night passed without incident. I readied myself for work and left Taylor sleeping on the floor. I met Eddie in the kitchen, on his way out to run laps at the track.

"He still here?" Eddie asked as we headed out the front door.

"Yeah. Sorry about it."

"'S'all right," he said. "Hey, could you show me or explain this friggin' school's registration process?"

"That's not until late August."

"I know, but if I gotta start checkin' on my scholarship money, then I oughta start now. This guy I met said it's a real fuckin' bitch of a system."

"Then I advise you to start checking on it now. Your friend is right." He laughed. We went our separate ways.

✵ ✵ ✵ ✵ ✵

We often live life between the rock and the hard place. Taylor's immediate needs were his problem, not mine. Was I being selfish to not want to help him? Yes. I could admit that. But when does helping, or just plain giving of

76

yourself, get old? What if it's not reciprocated? What about our ideas of reciprocation? That's all personal perception.

✱ ✱ ✱ ✱ ✱

Jill and Sue met me outside the restaurant after my shift. They invited me to go along with them to Zuma Beach. I thought that a day at the ocean would do my head good. Zuma was a nice beach, as far as Southern California beaches go.

We went back to my place, so that I might change. They could try and create a lunch out of whatever wasn't rotten in my refrigerator. Taylor was still there, sleeping soundly in my bed. This perplexed both Jill and Sue to no end. I just shrugged and said I'd explain it later. They set about hunting for food, while I shut myself in the bedroom to change into my swimsuit.

I stripped down in front of the dresser, then slid open the drawer. My swimsuit wasn't where it should have been. I was going through the rest of the drawers when Taylor awoke.

"Hi," he said with a froggish croak. He inhaled deeply and stretched like a much rested cat.

"Hi," I said as I made my way through the pile of clothes on the closet floor.

"What're you looking for?"

"My swimsuit."

"Oh," he said as if knowing something about it.

"'Oh' what?"

"I accidentally packed it with my stuff," he said.

I didn't say anything. I slipped on my pants and went out into the kitchen Jill and Sue were smearing peanut butter on bread.

"Slim pickings," said Jill.

"Got any jelly?" asked Sue as she licked peanut butter from the knife.

"Nope," I said. "I can't go."

"Why not?" said Jill.

"My swimsuit's gone."

"So wear cut-offs," said Sue.

"They make lousy tan lines," I said.

"Come on!" said Jill. "Improvise!"

"We can stop at one of those stores on the way to the beach," said Sue. "Pick up a new suit."

"All right, all right," I said.

"It'll do you good," said Jill.

I left them to their sandwich duty and returned to my room. Taylor was stepping into his pants. "You want me to go find it for you?" he asked.

"Forget it," I said as I redressed. "I'll pick up a new one."

"I didn't mean to take it."

"Look, Taylor, forget it. You've stayed as long as I can allow, okay?" He nodded. "Give Jay a call. He likes taking in strays."

"You rude fuck!"

"Maybe I am! But I'm not your fucking babysitter!"

Taylor's face flushed that pissed-off red. His body tensed, almost to a hard crack brittleness. He stormed past me and out the door. A moment later we all heard the front door slam. Jill peeked into my room.

"Trouble?" she asked.

"This time," I said, "we leave the strays at the beach."

*****

The sand burned my feet. The temperature had risen at least ten degrees since we left my house. There wasn't even so much as a hint of a breeze. Hundreds of bodies were sprawled along the shore like so many corpses from a shipwreck.

It'd taken us more than an hour to get there, including a stop at a surf shop along the way for me to pick up a swimsuit. Unfortunately for me, all this mini-emporium carried were Speedos. I chose a basic black one that covered as much of me as it could, but it still didn't feel like enough. I put my pants on over it and stuffed my underwear into my backpack.

I've had the same beach towel since I was seven. It was given to me when I began swimming lessons at the local YMCA. It was covered with stencilings of strange, abstract fish, now very faded from years of chlorine, washings and sunlight.

Jill and Sue found a neat little spot tucked away under a dune. We spread ourselves out like a housing development. They immediately fell into the sun bather's ritual. Baby oil glistened on their skin. Ray Ban's went on for the "cool" effect. These sun glasses would later be discarded to prevent racoon face.

I, however, was not so much a sun worshipper. I like the water. My inclination was to immediately dive into the waves. I did. Cool water. Murky water. Earth life that's tangible. I could never feel life in the soil, but I could in the sea.

I swam out to a chest level depth, then swam along the shoreline. There were few surfers left to impede my progress. The surf barneys and bettys usually came at six or seven in the morning, armed with wet suits, wax and Sea and Ski, to tackle the best waves of the day. I was free to swim, to float, to move. And I did move. Down to the bottom. Salty water stinging my eyes. Everything a brown hued green. Light. Alien sunlight refected on the surface, masking sight. The pressure of the water rumbled in my ears. Distorted sounds. I swept down to the ocean's bottom, then arced, then shot straight up to the light.

I didn't see him as I broke through the surface. My head just missed his fiberglass board. All I heard was a low, startled cry and a splash. The tip of his surfboard bounced over my head and plopped in front of me. He came up sputtering water and mild obscenities.

"Idiot! Watch where you're swimming!" His brown topped head stopped bobbing.

I tipped his board back to him. "Maybe you should surf on the sand instead," I said. "There were swimmers before surfers. We have the right of way."

He grabbed his board and stormed toward shore. "Fuckin' touristas!"

"I'm a native, qweeb head!"

"Then act like one!" he shot back. He marched out of the water. Idiot, I thought. I turned and swam back to the girls.

Jill and Sue were in the same position as when I'd left them. Face up under the broiler. I picked up my bath towel, not my beach towel, to dry off a bit.

"Don't drip on us," said Sue. I shook my hair like a fresh washed dog. They squealed as the spray hit them.

"You butt head!" laughed Jill.

"I should've brought Maul along. She could show you how to do it right."

You two need to turn over anyhow," I said. A purple frisbee clipped my elbow then dropped at Jill's feet.

"Over here!" the voice called. We all looked to the "over here." A group, more like a gaggle, of surfer dudes. Four of them. The one brunette waving his hand high in the air was the same mouth monster who'd bit me in the water. Jill picked up the frisbee and flung it. It soared smoothly, climbing up into the sky. Over their heads. Kersplash. It went down in the drink. Two of the "dudes" chased after it. The other two clapped for Jill's wonderful throw. She took her bow adroitly. "Come on," the leader called to us. Jill and Sue grinned at each other and ran toward the guys. The blond who'd retrieved the frisbee sent it soaring. Sue caught it. Their game began. I sat down on my beach towel to watch. The leader was the largest. About 5'10". Not the most handsome, nor the most built of the four, though. He played with the group for awhile. He turned to me a couple of times, beckoning me to join them. I kept shaking my head "no." Mr. Leader caught it again. His toss had power. The frisbee cut through a sea of midriffs and sailed down the shore. The others scrambled after it, laughing.

Clomp, thud. He trudged-hopped up the beach to me. A spray of sand dusted my ankles.

"Come on, wayward," he smiled.

"Wayward?"

"You swam in my way. I floated in yours. We're even."

"I don't care for a catch," I said.

"Then what do you care for?"

"A nap."

"Antisocial, like my brother," he said.

"I've never met your brother," I said. "So, I won't

presume."

"Leland!" the chorus rang. His name was Leland. Odd.

"Gotta go," he said jumping up. He tossed me a "bye" and ran back to the group.

I stretched back on the towel, then rolled onto my stomach. The sun was a heating pad. An intoxicant. I didn't intend on napping, but my body said to do so. The fight produced an alpha state of mind. The proper state to be in at any given time. Half sleep.

They were not dreams, but rather, disjointed images flashing like a high speed slide show. Sliding by. You. Me. Jill. Taylor. Kurt. You. Sue. You. You in the pick-up. You in my bed. You in me. Taylor. His scar. Fahad. My scar. You again at Irv's. Masks at a masquerade. Indescribable. I had to fight my eyes open. Blinding white. My towel. A sandcrab was there. Dead. A dead exoskeleton, once the feast of a gull. Myskin was baking. The frisbee skidded, spraying sand in my face. His foot landed beside it.

"Sorry," he said. He. Again. Leland the Leader. He snatched up the frisbee and flung it. He laughed then seat dropped next to me. He had callouses on his feet. He addressed me by my name.

"You a clairvoyant?" I asked.

"Jill told me."

"Where are they?"

"Having fun."

"So am I," I said.

"Yeah," he said. "Burning."

"You're Leland."

"You have ESP?"

"I have ears." I rolled up on an elbow to face him. His nose was peeling a bit. I guess I hadn't really looked at him on his first visit. Brown hair. Brown eyes. His eye teeth were pointed like little fangs. His wet suit had yellow and blue stripes on the sides. "Why aren't you playing?"

"I'm tired," he said as he flopped onto his back next to me.

"You look like you live here," I said.

"You don't?"

81

"Closer to downtown."

"I knew that," he said. "The girls told me."

"Malibu or Ventura?" I asked.

"West Los Angeles," he said. "On Sawtelle. Couple of blocks north of Olympic Boulevard."

"Southland native?"

"Yep. You?"

"Santa Cruz."

"Cool waves. Cold water, though."

I flopped onto my back. I could never get comfortable lying on my back. Seemed funereal.

"You drive your friends here?"

"No. They drove me."

"Good," he smiled.

* * * * *

Jill and Sue weren't too pissed that I bailed on them. Leland's friends were more than adequate replacements for me. Jill still dated Steven, but she enjoyed the art of flirting.

Leland's car was appropriately named The Beast. A convertible 1966 Mustang, made up of a patchwork of parts. Red hood, green fenders, yellow doors, blue fenders - one light, one dark, and a black trunk top. The poor thing had no top, though. Just a tarpaulin in the trunk for rainy days.

We talked the usual bullshit on the drive back. He worked in a surf shop in Venice Beach through the summers then went back to UCLA come the fall. He'd started college in 1974. Now, almost four full years later, he'd fulfilled enough courses to rank him as a second semester junior. I was to be a junior that fall, too. This would also entail my declaring a major. He said to do something that was fun or interesting. Boredom would come later in the workforce.

His apartment building was one of those blah, square blocked, early '60's construction nightmares. A pale, pale blue. So pale as to be dirty looking. We parked in the bowels of the building, then ascended three flights of stairs to his hallway, then entered his apartment - number 312. I liked that number. I liked any multiple of three.

The apartment, itself, was a topographical map. Green

carpeting rolled like so many hills and valleys, leading to a sagging brown couch which butted up against a sky blue wall. Everything was some sort of earth shade.

"My parents' left overs," he said as we moved into the bathroom. A clean room, but very well worn. Chipped enamel, rust stains and rusting fixtures. "Wanna shower?"

"Me?" I said. "Or us?" He smiled as he skinned off his wet suit. The hair on his chest was slick with sweat. I let my palms water ski then navigate around to his back as I pulled him to me. I licked his sweat. Salty. Clean. Licked again, kicking off my shoes as he removed my shirt. My tongue ran like a rasp up under his neck. His chin tucked down. His tongue caressed mine. We welded into each others' arms. Eating eagerly. Chewing lips. Saliva flowing wet, then wetter. Probing tongues dove deeper in as teeth clinked and fingers wrestled free our remaining clothes.

We slowly edged into the tub. His erection pressed against my hip. He slid to his knees, gently biting me as he went down. Strong fingers kneaded my ass, spreading my cheeks. The head of my cock slipped into a moist encasement. His thumb pressed into my hole then out as he grabbed my ass cheeks and thrust all of my dick into his mouth, suckling on me like a hungry calf on an udder. Soft lips. Wet cat's tongue. I swelled to capacity, to the point of hurting. I eased myself from his mouth and pulled his face back up to mine. We kissed again. I heard, or thought I heard, water begin to flow, but then I felt the hot wet between our stomachs as urine spewed up from his uncut cock. It was a weird sensation. I kissed him hard. Real water ran, cold, spitting out from the shower head. We washed. I soaped his chest, his arm pits, his fuzzy ass, scrubbing his skin and massaging his muscles. A laundering of flesh. He had no smell, this one, by the time we were done.

We went from the bathroom to his room. All walls were a collage of men cut and clipped from magazines and photos. So many to the point of being none. Low shelves lined one wall, double tiers of pornography and drug related paraphernalia. Black out curtains, replicas of an intangible post-war period, evaporated the daylight. He flicked on a lamp. A dim red bulb ripened the room. He closed the door, then drew yet another curtain across the door.

He pointed to his bed. A futon, sheathed by a black sheet, was fitted into a frame that rested on the floor. One inch dowels extended out one inch at each corner of the frame. A small box was nearby.

We uncoiled ourselves onto his futon like a caduceus' snakes. He inched his way down my body, making his shoulders a lift for my spreading legs. He ate my cock. I felt my body levitate as he pushed himself up on his knees. He ate my balls, then buried his face into the crack of my ass.

His arm slid around, shoving a bottle of poppers under my nose. I inhaled the chemical scent. My temples pounded in four-four rhythm. The red of the room blended with electric blue flashes of carnal wantings. Wanting to loose the angel of hedonism. Wanting to loose all fear into abandoned pleasure in sexual acts.

The binds that tied were soft satin cording, ankle to dowel, ankle to dowel, wrist to dowel, wrist to dowel. An inarching of flesh and wood. Pinocchio's claim. He lay down beside me, sucked on a joint, then kissed me. Pot smoke swirled from the dragon's nostrils. I was lickerish, all submission, wanting to be taken. Again the brown bottle came up under my nose. Again an herb kiss. Again and again. Jet-fuel mellow. I lost all sense of common sense as my body felt the surge of flesh-lust crackle from the centre point of my crotch. I wanted all he could do. His tongue washed over me. His lips sucked and sucked. Teeth bit and bit. Forever. My tensed, arched body signaled the near explosion. He stopped. Drew that box up close. Smiled.

He withdrew each item from the box with ceremony. A can of warm soda. He popped it open and took a sip. Fizz fizzed. Then a bottle of baby oil was held aloft. Then a feather. Then a piece of folded up foil. He gently traced the square of foil over my erection before methodically unfolding the almost endless folds of silver. A pill was enclosed. He bit it in half, grinned, then took a mouth full of soda.

He crawled up on me, gave me another quick hit from the brown bottle, then kissed me. A gush of fizzing fluid filled my mouth. I could feel the dissolving half pill as I swallowed.

"Ludes, man," he said as he gulped down his half with another swig. "We're gonna get it right. Downright nasty." He held the bottle of oil high up over me, letting the dribbling fluid splat on my skin like bird piss.

The half lude fizzed in my stomach as the oil rained down warm and slick. I lay my head back as he painted the oil over my skin with his feather. Delicate ants in velvet boots stormed over me. His hands were kneading putty.

I was getting dizzy. Red glow and shadows made the cracked ceiling twitch. Twitch then revolve. Earth on a collision course with oblivion.

He brushed. He bit. He chewed softly, the caterpillar on the leaf.

"Completion, baby," he whispered. A soft, satin blindfold created the abyss of night. I fell in. The room blacked out. I tripped.

*****

A screeching gull rumbled in my brain. Cold sand meshed with my skin. I sat up wiping and spitting away a grey fog. All of me, haphazardly dressed, was there on the beach. I felt stings as I stumbled onto my feet. Some jogger approached.

"Are you all right?" She was older. Gray hair. Blue sweat suit. I fell back on my ass. "My God!" she breathed as she helped me back up. "I'll get help . . ."

"No," I croaked. "I'm all right."

"Were you mugged?"

I let out a half snicker, half cry. My chest, my stomach, exposed by the opened shirt, were a lattice work of bloodied, sand encrusted welts.

"Come along." She helped me limp up the beach.

I was in Venice. Did he dump me there, backpack and all? Did I dump myself? I didn't know. When the woman left me at a bench to go phone for an ambulance, I crept away.

Everything was still in my pack. I dug out some change and called Jill from a pay phone. No answer. I called Lisa. No answer. I even called Eddie. No answer. Digging around in my pack, I happened on Carl's number. Could I call him at that hour? I tried the others again. And again. No response. I called Carl.

***** * *

He wanted to take me to the emergency room. I refused. What would I have said to the physician? I took a lude and a trick did me down right nasty? I talked him out of it.

We went to his place, a comfortable, uncomplicated apartment. I showered. He washed my clothes for me, giving me his robe to wear in the meantime. I tied the belt tight, then let the top half slip down my shoulders and back so that Carl could apply ointment to the welts.

He didn't speak much. Didn't need to. His soft spoken abruptness let me know his anger and his disapproval. Making small talk would've been moronic on my part.

He capped the salve, pulled the robe back up about me, then had me sit on the sofa, a seven foot beige bed of velvety soft cotton pile. He sat on an ottoman, directly in front of me. His eyes would've made me swoon had I not felt like such an ass.

"Did you learn anything?" he asked.

"Not to turn control over to strangers," I said.

"So, why did you?"

"He . . .seemed okay. The last I remember, he was being gentle."

"Drunk? Drugs?"

I just nodded. He sighed. Almost a laugh. He rose and turned from me. The image of a father holding back his temper.

"I had no right to call you," I said.

He pivoted into me. A lunging jackal ready to rip into decayed flesh. He took a deep, deep breath. "I want . . .," he started, his fingers compressing into a rock of a fist, "to slap you. Knock that idiotic head of yours into tomorrow."

"That wouldn't be very loving." Whoops. Bad joke.

86

"No," he said. "It wouldn't. Kids like you scare me."

"I'm not a kid."

"No?" His rigid body slacked. He sank back onto the ottoman. "You allowed this."

"I got fucked up."

"Why?"

"Because I just did! It happened!"

"Are you campaigning for the sympathy vote? Adding another tale to your legacy of victimisation?"

"That's not fair!" I wailed.

"Pity me on my pity pot!" he said with a smirk.

"I didn't claw myself up, you shithead!"

"You call me for help, then you call me a shithead for helping. That's good." I got up abruptly. He shoved me back down. "Sit!"

"I'm not your fucking dog!"

"You let yourself be someone else's dog!" He reached in for me. Tore open the robe. I slugged his arms away. He yanked me to my feet, twisted back my arms as I kicked at him, then shoved me down the hallway into his room.

I felt myself getting erect as the robe flapped open. He slammed the bedroom door closed and flicked on the light. "You wanna fuck me?!" I yelled, ripping off the robe. "Then fuck me!" He whipped me around, shoved me at the full length mirror and locked my sight lines in with his hands.

"Look at yourself!" he yelled. I started to move. He grabbed my head and forced me to stare. At myself. At the welts from neck to ankle some now oozing fresh red, at the bruises, at the cigarette burns on my hip, at my wounded crotch - my cock all swollen and rubbed raw. I looked ugly. From puffy eyed head to blistered toe. The purity of grotesqueness. My knees gave way. Caved in on their jelly bones. I was too sickened to cry. A throat full of cactus gagged me.

He came up behind me, his arms closing about me as sturdy as branches but as soft as spring leaves. The jackal's howl unclenched my throat and I cried. He held me and I cried.

I awoke in his bed. The sheets hinted his cologne. His smell. Warm sheets. A gentle bed. Still my body ached. The cigarette burns stung like bees' barbed weapons were digging in to root. I felt worse inside. Guilt welled up for my having invaded this man's life. How sick of feeling guilty doesn't one have to get before he can vomit it out? Feeling this was worse than feeling dead.

He came with breakfast. Oatmeal, juice, water and vitamins.

I ate as he instructed while he sat in his corner chair, watching me.

"Why do you do this to yourself?" he asked.

"I don't know."

"Don't know? Or, don't want to know?"

"I do it . . . to keep from feeling dead," I said.

"There are other ways."

"You, Lisa, can see other ways," I said. "Look at a swamp. What do you see?"

"Reeds," he said. "And frogs. Snakes. Waterfowl, eggs, nests, growth . . ."

"What about the mosquitoes," I said. "What about the flies, the maggots, the shit, the general decay. Wherever there's life, there's the stench that keeps it going."

"You have a choice. Be the hatchling, not the rotting egg."

"Easy to say. Not so easy to be," I said.

"Maybe you thrive on abuse," he said. "Self-inflicted or otherwise."

"Maybe. Maybe fundamentalism and anarchy are too extreme."

"Most of us walk the middle."

"And who defines the middle, Carl?"

"Look," he said. "I can't make you like yourself. You have to do that. You have to want that."

"I wasn't asking you to."

"But you don't even want to try! Do you?!"

"Walking the middle? Or liking myself?"

"Shit!" he exploded. Body up. Arms flailing. Eyes bugged. "You are a shit! A sick shit who like comebacks and discussions and proving to yourself that you're right!"

"I don't!"

"And I call you a liar, sir! You do this because you're scared shitless that you're wrong! That there's worth to yourself and everything around!"

"What's the worth of misery?!" I felt my face flush hot.

"Then why don't you do us all the favor of killing yourself if you feel that way?! Save us the drama!"

Dirty dishes rained across the floor as I sprang at him, knocking him into the corner. I hit him a couple of times, I think. I don't know. It was over in an instant with him on top of me pinning me to the floor. Blood leaked from his nostril. I was scared. He panted heavily. Red drops dripped on my face. His eyes filled with wetness, then overflowed.

"I . . ." he started, "know what you want. You want me to rip you open wide! Open you up for the last time. The final time." He eased up. Stroked my cheek. "I won't do that for you. You know why? Because it's not really what you want. Is it."

I choked. He had kicked in my wall. My own dark space flooded out like a lanced, puss filled wound. He dismounted me, picked me up like an injured child and placed me back on the bed. I balled up into myself to cry. I wanted him to go away, but he didn't. He lay down beside me, like a parent would, drawing me to his breast to hide. His heartbeat was steady. Hypnotic. I fell fast asleep.

✳ ✳ ✳ ✳ ✳

The Santa Monica freeway was bumper to bumper. Carl didn't seem to mind. He used such times to listen to tapes. To reflect on the past and think about future callings. That's what he wanted me to do. To reflect. To think. Thinking gave me a headache. He turned down the volume of the classical tape that was playing and smiled at me.

"Why aren't you married?" I asked.

"I was once," he said. "She wanted different things."

"Like what?"

"Children."

"You would've made a good father."

"If I could've become one. Such is life."

89

"Adoption?"

"She wanted to experience childbirth."

"Haven't met anyone else since then?"

"I don't fall in love so readily," he said.

"Me neither."

"But nothing would make you happier, would it."

"I don't know," I sighed.

"What about . . .Rex was his name, right?"

"What about him?"

"Ah . . ."

The traffic started moving again. Glass, metal, concrete and asphalt. A moving mini-city of its own. So many people, yet I couldn't see any one, save Rex.

"He doesn't really want me," I said.

"Are you sure about that?"

"He won't give it a try."

"Meaning," he said, "he's scared, too?"

"I guess."

"Sometimes we have to let go of people, regardless of our interest."

"But in the past, he's the one who kept coming back to me."

"Again, you allow him to."

I sighed the sigh of the resigned. Carl was right. I allowed you to come back, always, because that's what I wanted. However, what I wanted was making me crazier than I'd ever thought possible.

I steered the conversation away from you and back on to Carl. He knew my manoeuvre but let me have my way. He was a good man, Carl. One I could've very easily let myself fall in love with. But, I knew I didn't need to compound my crap anymore with pursuing a straight man. I sat in my seat, stared ahead, chatted and scratched the itching welts.

✻ ✻ ✻ ✻ ✻

Eddie didn't question me at all. He just gave me phone messages he'd collected and went on about his business. Jill had called twice. Dina, Jay and Lisa. No Taylor. No you.

I couldn't lie to Jill about what had happened. She and

Steven wanted to come over to talk about it, but I begged off. I told her that Carl had talked me out. She accepted my choice without our usual flack. I negated Dina and Jay's messages. I had to work the next day. I wanted to sleep. But I felt obligated to return Lisa's call. I was afraid she'd be upset about my having imposed on her uncle as I had.

She was home when I called. I hinted around a bit about the previous day's goings on, but it was soon evident to me that Carl hadn't called her. Being as perceptive as she was, she understood my dance of discourse. I decided it best to let her know the base facts of the matter, but not the details. She, too, let me off without further inquiry.

My bed was uncomfortable. I was uncomfortable. The weight of the battering I had allowed my body to be subjected to demanded a course of decision. Images cluttered my mind, pushing away sleep. Rick's clumsy mauling. Fahad's attack. The constant pointless fucking. The arguments. The vagrant on the beach kicking the Blue Nun out of me. To the point of nausea. Being parked under a transit bus would've been far more pleasant by comparison.

I got up and rummaged around for aid. All I could find were some stale allergy pills. Still, they were enough to make me groggy. Grogginess meant the possibility of passing out. Passing out would mean a mental and bodily shut down for the entire day. I unplugged the telephone and crawled back into bed.

*****

I was building a wall of brick. Mortar. Trowel. Brick. Mortar. Trowel. Brick. The wall kept falling. I kept rebuilding. I called into a void for help. Jill came. Sue came. Others. Taylor, Jay, Dina, Dan, Kurt, even Maul all came to help me build the wall. The urgency of completion fostered a solidification, turning us into rhythmic machines. We piled brick on mortar over and over. The wall grew. It grew high. Then crumbled at our feet. The machine panicked. Faster went our pace. Faster and faster. Build and rebuild. And just as fast did the wall topple, blown over by a gentle breeze full of fluttering rose petals. The others first froze in

91

horror at the sight. As petals wafted down upon them, the machine loosed a silent scream of agony and ran. Far from the wall. Far from me.

*****

My head felt like an onion being peeled. Questions and answers, questions and answers, them hoping to get to the core of my mind-fucked behaviour. But, what's at the core of an onion? More onion.

Jill and Sue gave me the phone numbers of their shrinks. Psychology, psychiatry, therapy . . . It was all the same to me. Stitches, casts, even inoculations, I could understand, could feel, could see the symptoms fixed within a relatively short period of time. But what of a mental state? It's neither solid nor gas. It wasn't substantial to me. Besides, a shrink would dare to go where no man has gone before. I didn't much care for the thought of that.

I filed these numbers away in a drawer. If I could have remembered Leland's address, I would've sent them to him. Anyhow, Lisa didn't come forth with the phone numbers of M.D.'s, Ph.D.'s and the like. She was just glad that I'd gone to Carl for help. She suggested that I visit him more, but pride and embarrassment made me fearful.

I decided it was best to keep myself busy for a time. No parties, no outings and definitely no more chance encounters. The life of a hermit, though boring, is much, much safer than that of a screwed-too-tight malcontent.

Weeks passed as the new school year slipped into place. I claimed Theatre Arts as my major. The drama group, of which Jill was a tangible part, seemed more stable in their insanity. And more familial. The breeder half were secure enough to hang with the queers. Interesting dynamics. Classes in this department made me forget about Taylor, about you, for a time.

I wasn't into the acting gig at all, but the classes were entertaining. I found my forte to be sets. I loved the illusion of creating a space, a place in time, that would not be permanent and I didn't have to haggle with actors' fragile egos. Just me and the other crew members, having a good time sawing, hammering and painting away.

✳ ✳ ✳ ✳ ✳

Toward Thanksgiving, we were working on a production of *Mrs. Warren's Profession*. Though the play wasn't going up until after Bird Day, we were loading in the set to hold tech rehearsals. It was on one of those days that you appeared in the wing space - a splice from the wrong movie.

I was quite astonished to see you there, proffering your hand and a smile. I had to stand my ground. I refused to even set down the chair I was carrying. Those few seconds of eye contact seemed like hours. You finally slid your hand back into your pocket and glanced at your shifting feet.

"What're you doing here?" I said.

"I had to see you."

"How did you locate me?"

"Talked to some people," you said.

"Lisa?"

"No . . .," you said. "Just people."

"'Had to see you'. That's what you said."

Jill arrived just then, all chatty and unaware. Her face whitened at the sight of you. No more chatty. She took a long, hard look at us then gently squeezed my shoulder. I nodded an acknowledgement. She understood and left.

You took the chair from me and set it aside. I couldn't move. I was transfixed by a mucilage of emotions to that moment in time.

"You're angry," you said.

"I've nothing to say."

"Taylor tracked me down."

"Taylor?!" My voice resonated in the fly space. I could feel confused eyes glaring, staring and waiting.

"Could we talk?"

"Now?!" I was beside myself. "Not now! Haven't you got eyes?! I'm busy!"

"What time, then?"

"Rex," I said, "it's been too long."

"Just a few months."

93

This time, it was your face that sank. "Good-bye" was like swallowing a rusted butter knife. I reclaimed the chair and left you standing there.

Jill caught me down right on the stage. She pulled me aside. I couldn't see her very clearly, though, for the blurring tears I refused to release.

"What'd he want?" she asked.

My voice, my mouth, failed me. The answer that came out sounded like that gagging gurgle that precedes vomiting. Jill sat me down in the chair. Some others who happened by us inquired about my health, suggesting that I go home before someone had to mop up puke. Her brief period of mothering ended with the director's intervention. He released me for the remainder of the evening.

I hadn't escaped you, though. You were there, in the parking lot, sitting on my car. You were huddled into yourself to ward off the chilly, night air. You looked up at me.

"Do you hate me?" you said. The lamp light and moon light glistened on your wet cheeks. I didn't think I'd ever seen you cry before.

"No," I said.

We climbed into my car. I turned on the heater. Cold air blew in. I turned it off.

"I'm parked on Exposition," you said.

We rode in silence. I double parked by your pick-up. You didn't move.

"Meet me at my house," I said. You nodded and got out. My head failed me as I drove back home. It spoke nothing to me. A complete theta trance of buzzing emotions and no conscious thought.

I parked and sat on the front porch, waiting. Waiting longer. Even longer. Finally your pick-up pulled up against the curb. Lights out. Engine off. The passenger door opened. You waited inside. I blindly accepted your offer.

I felt trapped with my executioner. We said nothing for the longest time. I looked everywhere except at you. You had that smell again. Apples. Always apples. Your breath felt warm on my neck as you closed in, turning my head with a gentle hand, bringing my mouth to meet yours. Such gentle, supple lips. Your saliva tinged with peppermint. A cool, soft kiss.

I agonized in that moment, as if you were slipping a noose around my neck. Your hands, still rough, felt my face. I wanted to embrace you, to devour you like a jackal's kill. I stopped you. And myself.

"You want to make me a madman, don't you?" I said.

"You're blue," you said.

"Why'd Taylor track you down?"

"He was angry with me."

"He doesn't even know you."

"Michael, your ex, introduced us at the Odessy. We talked for a time. He called me some months later in a fit because you didn't take him back. Said it was all my fault."

"That was some time ago."

"I know," you said. "I had a lot to think about."

"Like what?"

"Me."

"Bully," I said.

"And you," he said as he started the engine.

"What're you doing?"

"I want you to see where I live."

✲ ✲ ✲ ✲ ✲

We drove in silence up Hoover, to the freeway, then all the way to Lincoln Boulevard in Santa Monica.

"Where is it?" I asked.

"On Dudley."

You turned into a narrow alley and parked at the rear of the house. You got out of your pick-up. I headed toward the rear gate. You stopped me.

"This way . . ."

You took my hand and led me west, to the beach. Back at Venice Beach. Fog milked the blackness and muffled the sounds of the soft, lapping waves. We sat on the damp sand.

"I've had enough of beaches," I said. "They depress me."

"Me, too," you said.

"Look," I started, "You made your choice quite clear to

me months ago. Since then, I've been kicking you out of my mind, hoping the memories would finally run away."

"Did they?"

"They had, 'til you popped up tonight. You piss me off, you know that?"

"You scare me," you said.

"Me?!"

"Yeah, you."

"If I do, it's because you make me insane."

"Why?"

"Because I was in love with you, you damned jerk!"

"Taylor was in love with you. You scared him, too."

"Is this about Taylor, or you?" I snapped. "I don't have the foggiest where this conversation is leading."

"It's about all of us."

"Let Taylor speak to me face to face, then."

"He can't. He's still in love with you."

"What about you?"

"Yes."

"And?" You just shrugged. I stood up, wiping the clumps of sand from my backside. "Fine. I scare you both. Well, I didn't come with you to discuss my psychotic personality. Why don't you just forget it, once and for all."

"Flies buzz around honey," you said.

"They go mad over shit, too!" I could feel the wall in me rising at an alarming speed. "Which am I?"

"Which am I?" you asked.

"Take me home, please," I said. You sighed and nodded. I hated that sigh. It seemed exasperated. I wanted you to pursue the dialogue. You didn't . I could feel the tension between us as we walked back to your pick-up. You had a lot to say, but didn't. I did, too.

I didn't see that place where you lived. I didn't see anything on our long drive back to my house. You let me off at the curb and sped down the street.

✱ ✱ ✱ ✱ ✱

I found Eddie asleep in front of the television set. An emptied bottle of schnapps lay beside him. I turned off the

96

television, went into the kitchen, then pulled out my own unopened fifth of vodka from the freezer.

I drank the whole damned bottle, expecting it to put me out. It didn't. Whatever the reason, my tolerance was at a peak.

There's a queasiness that comes from too much drink. My stomach felt like Hiroshima after the A-bomb blast, yet I wasn't drunk. I thought, dying won't bother me, unless it's going to feel like this.

I fixed myself a solution of tepid salt water and gulped it down. Two more full glasses in a row. I felt the fluid churning, rumbling inside me like a forthcoming storm. I spent the next ten minutes glued to the toilet bowl. God got me for my stupidity. The vomiting gave me cramps. The vodka gave me cramps. God gave me cramps. I understood all too well what misery women must go through every month.

I took some aspirin and crawled into bed. No sleep, though. Just images. The mental slide show - of life as it felt, as I wanted it to be and how it really was.

I kept seeing a pleasant home, worthy of a backlot set, with a green, green lawn and bushes of white roses. The house was a single story clapboard, painted white. A very handsome home. I mowed this green, green lawn, happy in my work. Happy with this sanctuary. Then they would appear, Rex and Taylor, each carrying intangible balls of burning light. They blew on the lights, much as children would joyfully blow milkweed seeds to scatter in the wind. These fluffs of light floated into the house through clean, open windows.

Orange burned within the house and I watched as the clapboard buckled and melted like plastic in an oven. I was dumbstruck, unable to act. Taylor and Rex picked up a garden hose and aimed it at the melting house. Flames spewed from the hose, feeding the fire and hurrying its destruction of my home.

The next thing I knew, I was standing on a smoldering lawn, ashes clinging to my body's sweat. Everything was gone. Cinders and smokey residue for the ash can man.

97

Rex and Taylor were gone.

My body transformed, turning canine. Fur bristled. Smells became acute. Their smells. The smell of self-preservation. It was a surreal image worthy of Hollywood's special effects. I became the jackal, scenting for the kill.

I didn't like this image, which was quick in its execution in my mind. I forced myself out of the bed, lighted a cigarette and went into the kitchen to brew a pot of tea. Eddie's spastic snoring echoed through the house. I realized that I hadn't really taken the time to get to know this lodger. I didn't really want to. He didn't need me in his life, nor did I need him in mine.

The tea was flavourful, but a half a mug ignited my stomach. I dumped the rest out, then took a shower, hoping hot water and steam would relax me. It only served to wake me further. Frustrated, I went through the entire medicine cabinet, reading all the drug bottle labels in search of one that would promote drowsiness. I found some decongestants and popped the recommended dosage. It worked. Finally sleep. A dead sleep.

*****

I awoke at eleven the next morning, my sinuses pounding their disapproval. I'd missed my geology class and lab. Oh well. Day after tomorrow would be Thanksgiving. I had opted not to go home for the holiday, as I had wanted to use the time to cram for exams. Monday was to begin the cycle of tests and performances of the Shaw play.

*****

Holidays spent alone are misery. Eddie went home for the entire Thanksgiving break to be with family and to glut himself with fine, nutritious foods. Me, I found company with my text books, reading information I knew would be long forgotten by the coming spring. This aspect of study is odd, as it seems futile to pursue.

My family telephoned me that Bird Day, which only reinforced the hollow feeling inside me. I wished that I had not been so stubborn in my choice to remain behind. I knew then that I didn't want to be alone that day, so found my address book and began dialling numbers. Jill, Steven and Sue had all gone down to Newport Beach. Jay, Dina, Clark, even Michael were all gone. I tried Lisa's number. Her very novel answering machine was the only presence I found. I even toyed with the idea of calling Taylor, but my mind suggested that would be folly. And you, after I'd treated you so terribly the other day, I was sure that you would just as soon have spit in my face as to see me. I tossed the address book aside. I was deflated, but I had to do something, even if by myself. I had to be around people.

✳ ✳ ✳ ✳ ✳

I drove down Sunset Boulevard to the Tiffany, a one time legitimate theatre that now played movies, including a standard midnight showing of "The Rocky Horror Picture Show."

The Tiffany was playing some German movie about a man and a youth who have a weird love affair while in prison. It was the sort of film that suited my mood. I paid the admission, gawked a bit at the employees, a gangly group of New Wave and Fiorucci mix, then headed into the auditorium. Only a baker's dozen bodies were slumped down in seats. The lights went out. The movie began.

It wasn't long before I felt a presence slink into a seat near mine, rustling and crunching popcorn and obnoxiously slurping down a soda. I took a peek at this intruder, though I couldn't make out much more than the figure of a man intent on eating and watching the screen. Luckily for me, his voracious chomping and gulping didn't interfere with my ability to read the movie's subtitles.

The film finally ended, its story leaving me more depressed. I sat reading the German credits as they silently rolled up. Others quietly left the theatre. Finally the lights came back on. The theatre was empty. Or, so I thought.

"Marvellous movie!"

I turned my head. The mad muncher was still there. On a quick take, he was attractive, rather like a young version of Peter O'Toole. He had a very broad smile and very sad eyes.

99

"Depressing though," I answered as we both stood up.

"Any movie might be depressing on a holiday such as today," he said as he followed me out of the row and into the aisle. "Especially if it's seen alone."

I shrugged an agreement as we entered into the lobby. I moved on. He stopped briefly to deposit his trash into a trash can, then slid into his rumpled overcoat and hurried to catch up with me.

Out on the sidewalk, he kept pace with me as I headed toward my car.

"I saw a most extraordinary Pasolini film the other day," he said.

"His films are wonderfully depressing," I said.

"There's a restaurant just down the street," he said. "Would you care to join me for a bite?"

I stopped and looked at him. A fine cross-hatch underscored his eyes. Green eyes. Deeper lines created by slowly aging cheeks made prominent his mouth, which broke into a great smile. Fine gray peppered his neatly cropped sandy hair. He was older than I'd first guessed, but he was handsome nonetheless. His speech had the faintest hint of foreign influence. His smile did melt me. I smiled with a rather embarrassing snort and agreed to his invitation with a nod.

✳ ✳ ✳ ✳ ✳

The restaurant wasn't crowded. The hostess, though, seemed miffed that the place was even open, for she seated us in an obscure corner booth. Our waitress, a no-nonsense but professionally polite woman, was evidently in the same frame of mind. She served us quickly and efficiently.

His name was Eric. He'd moved here from England some twenty plus years ago and found the Southern California climate to his liking. He worked in film distribution and had just recently purchased a condominium in one of the newer developments on Kings Road. His job sent him on periodic junkets to Europe which pleased him to no end and gave him many tales to entertain me with throughout our meal.

As we ate, I lead the course of conversation to keep him

talking more and me talking less. I felt it safer to let him expose himself to me, rather than I to him. He was a witty man. Pleasant and full of charm. I liked him.

We'd just begun our dessert when reality, in the form of Taylor, cracked the pleasant mood. The circumstances surrounding how he came to be in that restaurant at that particular time was of no concern to me. I just wanted him gone. No such luck. He pulled up an odd chair and parked himself at the table.

"Hello," he said to me. I groaned. He turned to Eric. "Is this your father?"

"Sorry," Eric said. "Just an acquaintance."

"Yeah," Taylor snorted. "I used to be one of his acquaintances, too."

"What do you want, Taylor?" I said.

"Just to say hi."

"You said it. Now good-bye."

"Have you heard from Rex recently?" he pressed.

"About a week ago," I said. "I don't recall ever inviting you to sit with us."

Taylor turned back to Eric. "He's always bitchy and rude to ex-lovers."

"I see," said Eric. "Perhaps he has good reason."

"He's not God. He's just as fucked up as the rest of us, but he won't admit it. Enjoy your dessert, gentlemen," he said as he stood up and marched off.

Eric let out a small sigh, then dug his fork into his slice of chocolate cake. My ice cream had already started to melt, so I pushed it aside.

"Would you prefer something else?" Eric asked.

"No, thanks," I said. "My appetite's been canceled."

He nodded. "I'd say that your young friend is still quite interested in you."

"I apologize for the disruption."

"It's understandable," he said.

"No it's not!"

"Please, let's not quarrel about it now. Perhaps it's time for 'your father' to say good-night. And to thank you for your company."

"That's it?" I said. "Dinner and good-night?"
Eric seemed surprised. "Should there be more?"
"Is 'more' what you'd like?" I asked.
"We're going to be cryptic now, are we?"
I smiled at him. "I haven't had my dessert yet."

✳ ✳ ✳ ✳ ✳

His condo was still full of half unpacked boxes and moving
cartons. Everything still reeked of newness. From the
virgin white walls to the unscuffed floors. The place was
still in search of its impending history.

He led me into his bedroom where we stripped down to
skin. I started to lay down on the bed when he said, "No."
He positioned me at the side of the bed as he sat on its
edge. Just out of arms' reach, he stared at me, studied my
body and face. He leaned forward a bit so that his
fingertips could gently steer my course. Around. All the
way around. 360 degrees.

"Beautiful," he whispered. I'd never been called
beautiful before. I thought it to be a rather uncomfortable
adjective. As I turned to face him again, I saw his body, his
cock, for the first time. He had a slight build. A smooth
torso and hairy legs. His flesh seemed loose and soft. His
nipples, pale to the point of near invisibility. He had a
normal size organ, but it was perfect in shape and texture.
No bend or sway in its shaft. No dark tones in the skin. No
rugged topography on its entire length caused by a
multitude of bulging veins. It had been such a long while
since I had sex with a man that hadn't been peppered with
drugs or emotion or kinky behaviour that I wasn't sure
what I was supposed to do.

I proffered my hand to him. He took it and gently pulled
me down on top of him. His flesh was soft and pliant,
scented with talcum. I very much liked his smell. My
finger traced his eyebrows, as downcast as a willow's
branches, that framed those bright green eyes. I hadn't
studied a man's eyes like that, nor had I been so captivated
by such eyes, in ages. Not since yours. He had your eyes.

"You've beautiful lips," he said to me as his finger traced

102

their outline. I slid his finger between their split, wetting it. He then stared into my eyes and traced his own lips with the saliva streaked fingertip. We kissed. Kissed again. Hands pressed each other's head and mouth together. He kissed my face, my neck, my hands, my mouth, chewing on my lips. He was a man starving for affection. Affection that I longed to give. Each time I looked into his eyes, I saw his sadness. My sadness. Your sadness. This drew me down his torso, my mouth and hands wanting to drive this sadness from the heart caged within him; down to his pelvis where a lifetime of guilt and pain quivered their release under my massage; down to his groin where his cock twitched in ready anticipation of its moist, warm receptacle -my mouth. His entire body arched as if he'd been shot in the back with an arrow as my lips spread over the head of his penis and the entire silky shaft slid down my throat.

"Please . . ." he uttered as he drew my head up from his crotch. His short, heavy breaths and burgeoning smile pleased me. I rested myself on him once more, cradling his temples between my palms, pinning his head down on the mattress. I licked his face lightly - all over - tracing eyes, brows, nose and mouth with the tip of my tongue.

His hands came up about me, clutching me, crushing me, to him. I rested my head on his shoulder, my nose regaling in the scent of his skin.

"Eric?"

"Hmmmm?"

I pushed myself up, then guided him up. "Lay on me," I said. I went down on my back. "I let you stare at me. Now, I want to feel your weight on me." He did so, letting his arms fold up across my chest to form a sort of chin rest for himself. His face glowed like a pup's.

"Better?" he asked.

"Better," I said as I studied his face and toyed with his hair. "Tell me something?" His eyes drew a curious expression. "What makes you so sad?"

"Sad?" he laughed. "I'm anything but sad at the moment."

"What about other moments?"

"You're a curious one, aren't you?"

"You're an attractive man, with wonderful stories and a great deal of warmth, I suspect. Yet you were alone tonight."

"So were you," he added.

"But, if you hadn't tagged me, I'd be back home right now."

"Doing what?"

"I dunno . . . I'd probably have taken the phone off the hook then cried 'cause no one was calling me." I'd thought that to be a joke, but he didn't laugh.

"I'd probably be doing the same thing," he said as he rested his face upon my stomach.

I gently entwined his hair in my fingertips and pressed his head to me. Looking down on him, at that angle, in the dimness of the room, he looked as you once did. You in a moment when you truly wanted me.

"What more would you like to do, Eric?"

"More?"

"I can understand the hollow in you."

He looked up at me. "Can you?"

"Do I remind you of someone?" I asked.

His arm reached up, his hand stroked me from shoulder to knee. "Would that be bad?" he asked. "I suppose it is. It's unfair."

I drew his other hand up and pressed his palm to my chest. "It's not bad," I said. "It's honest."

"Then, yes. You do remind me of someone from a very, very long time back."

"And you loved him?"

"I've been a prisoner for years now."

I slid my hands under his shoulders and drew his weight back up on me. I kissed him gently.

"Then make love to him tonight, Eric," I whispered. My legs slid up around his hips. I kissed him again, whispering, "Make love to him."

✳ ✳ ✳ ✳ ✳

I lay awake the remainder of the night. Eric was in a deep sleep beside me. The moonlight, bleeding in through the window, freckled the rumpled bedclothes with laciniate shadows - each imagined leaf pointing to a separate direction, like so many broken compasses. How should I navigate my course, I thought. Arise and run? Stay and see what the morning would bring? What would he prefer? What would I prefer? He'd made love to a fantasy and so had I. In the dimness of night's enviable light, I could see you in him.

✱✱✱✱✱

I must have nodded out as morning came, for my last recollection was of the sun's rays creeping in slowly through the window while a bird chirped for its morning meal. The clock near his bed read 10:43. A quarter to the hour and I wasn't yet gone - but Eric was.

I crept into my clothes and took a gander in the mirror to see what sort of creature I'd transformed into. Stubble, pillow head and puffy eyes. An unpleasant sight. The stubble could wait. The urgency was for a basin of water to pull my appearance together.

The bathroom was just across the brief hallway. I entered and locked myself in. It all looked newer than I'd remembered it. A shiny, gray commode and sink. Shiny chrome fixtures. The shower curtain faintly perfumed the air with its pungent, plastic newness. I washed as quietly as I could, taking care to leave the hand towel that I used seemingly virgin. The cool water helped revive my skin. A good, gradual dousing helped tame my wild hair, which, at that instance, seemed to me to look very, very thin.

"Good morning!" he boomed, his voice almost rattling the hollow core barrier of a door. "Are you hungry?"

"No," I said.

"Coffee, then?"

"Sure . . ."

I wasn't sure that he was gone, as the thick carpeting muffled his footsteps. When he didn't speak again, I assumed it was safe. I cracked open the door to peek out,

105

half expecting to be greeted by a Donna Reed wannabe. Nope. I was safe.

I padded down the hall into the living room. The only escape route was the front door, which, as fate would have it, was in direct line with the open end of the galley kitchen. God, how I hated the architect of that condo-confab at that moment. I just knew this design was deliberate to confound people like me.

It wasn't even a moment before Eric appeared in the small dining area with two mugs and a coffee pot. I strained a smile. He looked even better than he had the night before. I wanted to cut his heart out.

"Come, come . . ." he said.

"I'm a walking advertisement for the morning after, Eric. I should go."

"Don't be absurd," he said. "You look fine."

Maybe he didn't have his contact lenses in. Maybe the light was bad. I gave him the dreaded close-up by joining him at the table. He poured me a steaming mug of Kona. My face fell right into it.

"I had the luxury of a shower and a shave," he said. "You can take a shower, you know."

"I'd just get dirty again."

"You sure you're not hungry?" he asked as he pulled a cigarette from the pack in his pocket and lit it.

"Yeah," I said, "but I could do with one of your smokes."

He handed me his cigarette, then lit another. "Nicotine and coffee," he mused. "Ghastly combination."

"I hate you," I said flatly.

"Based on what?" he said blandly.

"I won't look as good as you do when I'm your age."

"Do you always serve up backhanded compliments first thing in the morning?"

"It's been my specialty," I said.

"Do you wish that last night hadn't happened?" he asked. I shrugged. "I half expected you to be gone when I awoke this morning."

"I'd thought about it," I said.

"So?"

106

"I like you."

"Seems to me that there's more to it than that," he said.

"I wanted to be someone else for you last night, so that you could be someone else for me."

"And?"

"Dunno . . ." I said.

"We're a lot alike, I think," he said.

"How come you don't have a lover?"

"I told you. I'm a bit of a prisoner of the past. Someone past, specifically."

"Mine's becoming a 'past', too," I said.

"Do you know what we are?"

"Please don't say two ships."

"No," he laughed. "Two people with a common link who'll probably not meet again like this."

"You wouldn't consider becoming fuck buddies?"

"No," he said, "and neither would you."

I smiled. He was dead on the money. "Because," I said, "attachment pre-empts detachment."

"The headmaster gives you an A."

"But," I continued," I want you to know that I do like you very much."

"Intimacy is a bother, isn't it," he said.

"Maybe I just don't understand it," I said.

"It scares me, too," he said.

"Well," I rose from by chair, "thanks."

He smiled his smile and we hugged. I took one last whiff of his talcum scent then broke away. He walked me to the door.

I still wanted more. I turned to him, stroked his cheek gently, then led his mouth to mine for one last kiss. His arms embraced me. I wanted to cry and I wasn't even sure why. Two more quick pecks, then I left, never looking back.

I thought long and hard about this encounter on my drive back home. I still couldn't figure it out. What toilet was I flushing my life down?

❋ ❋ ❋ ❋ ❋

Turkey Day rolled easily into Christmas vacation.

Christmas spent at home with the family up in Santa Cruz. Family duties kept my mind off of the mess I was making out of my life, off of Taylor, off of you. Then the festivities ended and my Dad toted me up to the airport to fly back down to Los Angeles, to New Year's parties, to the final classes and final exams of the Fall Semester, to my impending twentieth birthday.

January began. January, 1979. I had stayed in on New Year's Eve and New Year's Day. Classes were rolling on the second. I wanted to make up for my lagging grades by knocking out some high marks on finals. I did just that. Almost.

I finished my last final on the thirtieth. My twentieth birthday. It was a geology class, something I had little use for or interest in. My brain, depressed with turning twenty, failed me miserably. I knew I was going to end up with a C in the course, if not worse. That would play havoc on my G.P.A. Even with the credits I'd acquired in the summer of '77, I was still a first semester junior. I had wanted to be done with college in three years, get out and maybe, with a great grade point average, quickly enter into Graduate School. So much for the best laid plans, as they say.

To compound my depression, when I went home that late morning, Eddie informed me that he'd pledged a fraternity and would be moving out of the house by the next month's end.

My friends insisted I needed cheering up. They dragged me out to the Odessy for a fun filled night of dancing. They had a fun filled night. Me, I sat on the sidelines, stewing in a blue funk. Jay and Clark, higher than high on God knew what, tried to coax me out onto the dance floor more times than a millipede has legs. Their good intentions became so annoying that I had to flee to the patio for privacy among strangers.

Sue tagged me out there. She handed me her drink and leaned against the wall. She looked as bored as I felt. "You're not having fun," she said.

"No."

"Jill's bopping with Steve and the others."

"I'm glad they're having fun."

"You hungry?" she asked.

"Not really."

"Come on," she said. "Let's go to Jan's for grub."

"That's a plan."

*****

The usual patrons filled Jan's deluxe coffee shop - strange people and policemen. Sue and I were stuck in a window booth, she eating a club sandwich and me playing with a plate of deadly french fries.

"I know how you feel," she said. "I'm gonna be twenty next month."

"At least you've got a direction. You're nice. You know what you want to do," I said as I buried the grease sticks under a mountain of salt.

"Nice?" she snorted. "Nice gets you nowhere, you know. Jill's not always nice. She makes waves. She's bossy. She's blunt. Men chase her."

"Jealous?"

"Envious," she said as she stuffed the tail end quarter of the sandwich in her mouth.

"Me, too."

"Wha . . ." she started, then stopped to swallow. "What're you gonna do about Eddie?"

"Maybe it's time for me to move," I said.

"To where?"

"Around here, maybe."

"Change might be good, but can you afford to live alone? I mean, rents around this area aren't cheap."

"I can try," I said. "Maybe if I look hard enough, I'll find a good deal. I'd like to live alone for awhile, like Lisa does."

"Lisa Kanton?"

I nodded. "She's got a great studio down by school. I got a week before the next semester starts. I'll start looking tomorrow."

"Good luck," she said as she raised her glass of milk. "Let's hope twenty's better than anything before."

*****

Lisa called me the following morning at nine, blasting me out of a sound sleep. Carl had invited her to lunch. She said that he'd suggested that she invite me along. I was a little uneasy about it. I hadn't seen or talked to Carl in months, since the day he dropped me off after my encounter with Leland.

"Come on," Lisa coaxed over the phone. "That was then, this is now."

"Embarrassment can be terminal," I said.

"He likes you. He'd really like you to come."

"All right," I said. "When?"

"One o'clock. Swing by and pick me up at twelve-thirty."

*****

Carl still looked as attractive as he had that first time we'd met. His eyes and his smile, both jocose and energetic, relaxed me. Lisa had saved me by keeping the conversation directed — metaphysics, philosophy, future plans. I felt very secure; a child tucked between Mom and Dad during a thunder storm. Finally, Carl raised his glass.

"To your birthday," he said to me.

"Thank you."

"Your wishes shall come true," Lisa said.

"Wishes are for those under ten or over forty who still sleep with teddy bears," I said.

"Why must you do that?" she asked.

"What?"

"Kill everything?"

"I don't know," I said, suddenly feeling like Hitler at a barmitzvah.

"Tell me something," Carl interjected. "What would make you supremely happy on this day?"

"Dunno . . ." I said as I tried to think.

"No?"

"Well . . ." I said. "To not feel as I so often do."

"But you don't seem to want to change that," said Lisa. "You're running around unhappy more often than not. Sometimes I get the impression that you actually like depression."

"I don't think I do," I said. "But, it is what I know best."

"Depression? Or fear?" Carl asked.

"I thought it was all fear?"

"It is."

"So? How do I change that? Medication? Pop some lithium and get on with life?"

"Perception," Lisa said. "Perception."

"So?" Carl said again. "What would make you happy today?"

I didn't have to think about that one. I reached into my pocket and pulled out that piece of plate, that shard of pottery that I'd deemed to represent your heart. "Rex," I said.

Carl took the piece from me, examining it as a paleontologist might examine a stone in the desert. "What's this?" he finally asked.

"His heart," I said.

"You carry around a representation of his heart?"

"Kinda stupid, I know."

He set the shard in my hand. "Not really," he said.

"But," Lisa said, "what if it's not you that he wants? What do you do then? Continue on with depression and self-abuse?"

"I'm not used to getting what I want," I said.

"But you've been trying to change that, haven't you?" she asked.

"How do you mean?"

"Your last episode, when you ended up at Carl's, was some time ago."

I felt my face run red. "Yeah," I said. "But keeping a low profile has become rather boring. I don't do much of anything anymore."

"Why do you talk as if it's about 'doing' anything?" she asked.

"I don't follow."

"All right," she said. "What do you mean by 'doing'? Going to parties? Having sex? Getting obliterated on drugs? Alcohol?"

"What do you want me to say?" I said. "That I have a grand old time sitting home watching reruns? I don't. But

I'm really not very good with people."

"Let me suggest something," Carl said. "Why don't you try, without drugs or drinking or sex, meeting Rex again. Perhaps he has his own fears, too."

"I don't know, exactly, how to get hold of him," I said.

Silence. Lisa and Carl glanced at each other. I felt a set-up coming.

"He's still attending my lectures," Carl said.

I let out a sigh. "I see," I said.

"You said once that you wished you could be more like me," said Lisa. "To not be unhappy."

"What if he really doesn't want me?" I said. "I don't know how I'd deal with that. Sometimes not knowing is a hell of a lot easier than knowing."

"Just try," said Carl. "Tuesday night. Come with Lisa."

I nodded.

✴ ✴ ✴ ✴ ✴

The meeting was well attended. More earthy-crunchy types milling about spouting cosmic well wishing and profound friendship. Lisa and I sat in the back again as Carl took to the dais and began his talk. My eyes kept scanning the room, looking for him. For you. Why weren't you there? They said you'd be there. Did you screw up their plans? Did they make this up to keep me in line?

Carl must've talked for at least forty-five minutes and I didn't hear even one minute of his talk. My demon tapes were rattling and prattling around in my head. The break came. I excused myself to go out to the steps and pollute my body with another cigarette. Lisa let me go with ease.

The night air smelled clean. Tufts of smoke plumed up from my cigarette as it burned idly. I was tired. Tired was fast becoming my middle name. It was scary to just sit there, in the dark, realizing that there wasn't anything to think about. I'd exhausted myself.

"Hi," you said. My heart skipped a beat. I didn't move. You sat down on the step, next to me.

"I've missed you."

"Same here," you said.

112

I flicked the cigarette butt out onto the pavement. Your hand slid up onto my knee. I felt myself, my organ, straining a response.

"I'm an asshole," I said.

"Why?"

"Fear. I know you intimately, yet I don't know you at all."

"Intimate strangers," you said. "I think that's what they call it."

"Yeah," I said. "Or, like the way a wild animal's intimate with its prey."

"Is that what I am to you?"

"I don't know," I said. "Possibly."

You shook your head in understanding and stood up, stretching an invigorating stretch. You extended your hand to me. I took it and walked with you in the parking lot.

The fog rolled in, cloaking us with night's fichu. We lay in the bed of your pick-up truck, staring at the void of night. Fog distorts sound. Distant passing cars sounded dangerously close. Close footsteps never sounded at all. Still, no one bothered us there as our hands interlocked.

Your energy radiated. Permeated me. An infusion. A transfusion. Correct feelings. It's impossible to understand how one person can make everything seem all right for another by simply just being. You did that for me.

"What about fears?" you finally asked.

"I'm afraid of the possibilities."

"So am I."

"Am I too needy?

"Not that," you said. "Not quite that, anyway." You sighed deeply and looked at me, into me, with those penetrating eyes of yours. "Sounds stupid," you said, "but, I think I love you. That scares me."

"I do love you, you know."

"Do you? Really?"

"Yes."

"How can you know if it is love?" you said. "Maybe it's something else."

"I can't answer that."

"So, you really still don't know," you said with a sigh.

"I know that I want to be with you tonight. All night. I've still never seen where you hide."

You turned to me. A slight smile. Those eyes melted me into the sea. I wanted you right there. Anyone who might happen by, who might see us in the very act, could smile or frown or faint dead away for all I cared. I made my move. We kissed. Kissed long. Kissed hard. You hit the brakes.

"Not here," you said.

"I'm sorry. All I can seem to do when I'm with you is to devour you with every sense I have."

"You're blue tonight," you said as your hand stroked my cheek. "I'll come to you tonight. Just before dawn."

"Why not now?"

You pressed a finger to my lips, quieting me. My pavis hide made buttery soft by the reassurance in your smile. If being in love meant being able to stare at someone for infinite time, then I was dead in love with you.

We rose, climbed out of the pick-up and slipped back into the lecture. You moving to your side of the room and me taking my seat next to Lisa. She blindly targeted my hand with her own, giving it a thoughtful squeeze. She was pleased for me, I could tell.

✳ ✳ ✳ ✳ ✳

I left the front door unlocked for you. Ten o'clock came. Then midnight. Then three a.m. I couldn't stay away, nor could I sleep. Anxiety moved through me until I paralyzed. Fear's a great enemy. Finally, just as dawn insinuated through drawn shades, you entered my room with a lion's stealth. Poised before me, the golden light magnified your magnificent, naked form.

Once again you came to me, willingly, into my bed. Redolent of apple, you were more intoxicating than any drug could ever claim to be. Limbs welded in a soft tangle and we lay there, content to feel, until sleep stole away the morning.

Dreams of a single story home, green, green lawns and us, together, never aging, never again doubting, were slowly pushed aside as you woke me. I nuzzled into your side, my

114

nose delighting in your body's natural perfume. Your chest and stomach were the landscape before my eyes.

"Make love to me," I said.

"Make love with me," you said.

Shadows of former selves burned away in the intensity of our coupling that morning. Never before had I so profoundly experienced making love. Time did not exist. The world had stopped. All that was reality was you and me until we succumbed to bliss and blacked out until the following morning.

*****

The hammering on the front door wouldn't relent. Finally, I had to drag myself from your side, slip into my pants and stop this intrusion. Jill and Sue were at the door, all dressed in chic casual clothes.

"Aren't you ready?" Jill said.

"For what?"

"We're going to Laguna!" I stood there with the most dumbstruck expression on my face. "We made these plans last September!" she whined.

"I can't go," I said. Jill scowled. I fished around in my pockets and produced that fragment of plate she'd most likely forgotten about. "You once told me to forget him," I said. "I don't want to."

Sue looked beyond me, up the stairs. A curious smile broke across her face.

"Good morning, ladies." You were there, standing in your revealing briefs and wearing a pair of sunglasses.

"Hi," said Sue as she nudged Jill.

You came down a few steps.

"We're going to Laguna," Jill said. "You want to come with us?"

"Thanks for the invitation," you said, "but I think we'll pass."

Jill sighed and shot me an annoyed, but understanding look. I smiled at them. They tossed off their good-byes and climbed back into Sue's Falcon.

Your arms wrapped about me as I closed the door. You

licked my neck. My mouth craned around to swallow your tongue.

"Do you have to work today?" you asked. I shook my head. "Then what say we go for a drive?"

"Not to Laguna."

"No, not to Laguna."

✳ ✳ ✳ ✳ ✳

We ended up in that alley behind Dudley in Venice Beach. Once again I was to see your home. This time I would not be so stupid as to start a fight with you.

We ventured through the microscopic rear yard into your ground floor apartment. It was a tiny space with the suggestion of a kitchen in one corner. The apple scent was noticeable.

"This is it," you said.

"I like it."

"It's tiny, but cheap."

"What is it that you do, anyhow?"

"For work?"

"Yeah," I said.

You shuffled a bit. "Lots of things. Bartended, worked as a pipe fitter. Lots of things."

"Now."

"I drive for a courier service," you said as you sat me down on your full bed. The tangle of sheets and rumpled spread indicated it hadn't been fully made in quite some time.

"You're a restless sleeper," I said.

"When I'm here. It's usually daytime. I have a hell of a time sleeping in sunlight."

The phone rang. It seemed to jar you. You watched it ring and ring and ring. It wouldn't stop. You answered it and turned from me to mumble into the receiver. Your body language indicated a need for privacy. I stepped back out into the shade of that tiny yard and lit a cigarette. Your voice travelled. I couldn't understand much of what was being said. I finished my smoke long before you came out to fetch me. Your face had grown sullen. You barely glanced at me.

"I have to go," you said.

"Where?"

"To work."

"Oh . . ." I said. You put your arm about me and escorted me back to your pick-up. We climbed in and drove away.

✳ ✳ ✳ ✳ ✳

"I know how it is to be called in at the last minute," I said. You barely nodded. "Tell me," I went on, trying to break the mood, "why do you always smell faintly of apples?"

"Apple scented soap," you said. "I like it."

When we got back to my place, you assured me that you'd be back. I believed you. As I moved from the cab of the pick-up, you grabbed my hand and squeezed it with dead earnest. I smiled.

"What?"

"I don't want to let you go this time," you said.

"Don't," I said. You let me go. I climbed out and waved to you as you drove away. Your parting words were more important to me than a thousand meaningless 'I love you's.' I held on tight to that confession.

I fell on my bed, inhaling our scent of sex from the sheets. I wanted to weld this warp and woof to my skin. Hours went by as I lay on that bed. I became restless. I tried to indulge in a book, but reading would not command my full attention. I dug up a two old day newspaper to scan ads for apartments to rent.

I fell asleep. You didn't come back that night.

✳ ✳ ✳ ✳ ✳

I was two weeks into the Spring Semester; two weeks in a blue fog, before I heard from you again. You tracked me down and caught me after one of my fencing classes at the gym. I didn't bitch, didn't yell, didn't even posture for a fight. I stood and stared at you. You knew what I was feeling. I was sure of that. I could tell you were sorry. Very sorry. Apologies were chiselled in your eyes.

We walked to a quiet bench on the private green between

117

the gym and the auditorium. We sat silent for a moment as the few passers-by made their way to other parts.

"What can I say," you said.

"You tell me."

"I do care."

"Is there a problem?" I asked. "Tell me."

"What would be the point in that?"

"Come on," I said as I took your hand.

"Don't you have a class?"

"My professor's cool. He understands about scheduling conflicts."

We walked south to Exposition Boulevard. We crossed the street, then headed into the rose garden. The bushes were lush with new leaves and buds just beginning to form. We strolled for a time, my eyes staring at our feet as we walked. You stopped. I stopped.

"This is pretty," you said.

"Lisa and I had a long talk here once."

"Don't really know her," you said.

"You seem to know her uncle."

"He's an interesting man. I like what he has to say."

"He's helped me to the point of embarrassment," I said. You sighed, lifted your head and nodded toward the campus. "What?" I said. "You want to go back?"

"I don't feel right there," you said.

"I know it's not such a great neighbourhood, but . . ."

"Not that," you interrupted. "The neighbourhood's fine. It's the school."

"I don't get it."

"You're all there, trying to find your way in life."

"Everyone takes his own route," I said. "None of us know if he's doing it right."

"Knowing's one thing. Doing is another. You're doing."

"I'm blundering through," I said. "Times none of it feels right."

You looked at me with a quizzical expression. "You don't get it," you said.

"What am I supposed to get?"

"There's your opportunity," you said. "That school.

You've still got time to meet new people and make decisions that will affect you for the rest of your life."

"So? We all make choices."

"I'm not a part of that world, though. I can't offer what that entity has to offer."

"You offer more than that," I said.

"We're really different. Don't you realize that?"

"No, I don't. I don't come from an academic world. My parents, my grandparents, hell, no one in my family comes from this world. It was alien to me."

"But you belong to it now."

"That's for me to assess, not you."

"You'll get bored with me," you said.

No, I thought. Hadn't Taylor said something like that to me once? I couldn't remember clearly. Your remark hurt me, though. My sincerity felt challenged.

"Bored," I said. You glanced at me briefly, allowing me to truly see the fear hidden beneath your eyes. I wanted my bricks back. My wall. To protect me. I turned to a rose bush, seeking out its softness. Something to focus on. Something to soften me. "Is that fair?" I said. "You're pre-judging my actions."

"You got bored with Michael. You got bored with Taylor," you said.

I ripped a leaf from the rose bush, crushing it in my fisted up hand. "Michael?" I said. "Taylor?"

"I talked some to them," you said sheepishly.

"And they told you their side," I said. I felt the bricks piling quickly, compressing down into an extremely sturdy wall. The jackal contained by that wall wanted to burst forth and rip out their souls. I leashed the animal and threw aside the trowel. I turned to you. "I don't need to think about this. Bored is the one thing I've never been with you."

"You don't know me."

"You won't give me that chance."

You stood there, stammering. The sounds of a toddler unable to form a cry for help; unable to cry from fear.

"It's me," you said.

119

"You're apprehensive. I can understand that. We can take more time."

"There's a woman," you said. The wrench in the plans. The missing piece of the puzzle. The obvious overlooked. This would not register in my mind. "I love her, too," you said.

"Where," I said. "Where is she."

"She lives down in Norwalk."

"This isn't a joke, is it," I said. You shook your head. I could've dealt with this better had you been fucking Taylor, or Michael or any other guy. A woman was worse than unfair. I turned away and stared at the clouds. "I can't . . ." I said.

"You have to make this choice."

"I love you both."

"You can't!" I shrieked. "It's not fair to her or me!"

You sat on the ground, toying with your shoe laces, saying nothing. The rose garden proved to be a lie. No miracles. No magic. I wanted to bury you and me right there. Bury us under the roses.

"So," you said. "You're offering all or nothing?"

"What do you want me to say?"

"She doesn't know about you," you said. "She's pretty. She's nice. She's comfortable to be with. We laugh a lot. Talk a lot. There's no strain. She makes me feel peaceful." You looked up at me. "Then there's you. With you, there comes an intensity. A desire. An emotional upheaval that makes me feel so much a part of the living world."

"The sum of the two makes your world complete," I said. "Is that how it is?"

"Something like that."

"God," I sighed. "Fuck me naked. Fuck me dead."

"I used to imagine living with the both of you," you said. "It was a wonderful fantasy."

"Right. The Madonna and the whore. Guilt free sin."

"I suppose."

"And what do this whore and that Madonna do in your fantasy when you're not around? Or was that the edited portion of the program?"

You sighed and rose to your feet. "No editing," you said. "That scene was never shot."

"Because you knew neither she nor I could act in it."

"Well," you said.

"What?"

"I said it. That's what I had to do. That's what you wanted to know."

"No," I said. "Not that."

We stood there for a length of time, disconnected. My bricklayer was methodically working away, skillfully rebuilding my wall - the wall needed to contain the flood of emotions that were swiftly welling up inside me. Should I try to change your feelings? Should I find out her name and telephone her to inform her of your perversion? What could I do to keep you, one hundred percent? I wanted a drink. I wanted to get loaded and react in any way I possibly could. I felt your hand gently grip my shoulder.

"I'm going to go," you said.

"Where?"

"Just go."

I turned to you. "That's it?"

"I think it best for now."

I calmly lit a cigarette, waiting for you to go. You lingered. "I thought you were going," I said.

"I'm sorry. I'd hoped . . . Well, you know." You nodded again and turned away. A few slow steps.

"Rex!" I called. You stopped. "You're not coming back, are you?"

"I don't know."

"I want you to."

"So do I."

"I'm here. Always."

My bricks contained the fire within me; the springing well of tears I refused to undam. I didn't want to let you go. Not like this. Not to let you return to some nameless woman who'd keep you close to her heart and safe from an antagonistic world.

Still, the depression within me bore itself in my eyes. You returned to me one last time and clutched me hard in

121

your embrace. I remained detached at that moment. You pulled back slowly, searching my eyes for an appeal which I would not grant.

You turned and walked off, leaving me with a bottleneck of emotions choking the very breath out of me. I waited until you were long gone before I walked back to the campus, back to that secluded area where Lisa and I had our picnic so many months before.

In the beginning, I had strained to keep myself from feeling dead, all the while killing myself with liquor, drugs and sex. I hadn't abused myself since my rescue by Carl, hoping that change, for the better, would be inevitable. Now I wanted to return to my old ways. Safe ways, I called them, for the hurt born under those conditions was by far less painful than the hurt I felt at that moment.

I remained there until twilight. The beautiful sky seemed to feel for me; sheltering me with a palette of deep colours. I walked the long walk back home.

Within a week, I found myself a new studio apartment in the West Hollywood area. I moved myself unaided. Multiple trips in my poor, old Maverick, over the course of a weekend, kept me busy. Kept me from thinking about you. A new address, and new phone number and much wanted privacy fostered an illusion of rebirth. I avoided my old friends as best I could for quite some time, giving them inventive excuses for my lack of attention to them. I found another job at a restaurant within walking distance of my new home. I even went so for with this "renewal" process that I inquired about transferring to UCLA. Still, none of these changes completely quelled my missing you.

✳ ✳ ✳ ✳ ✳

Jill finally tracked me down. She telephoned my parents and obtained from them my new phone number. She wasn't happy that I'd avoided her for so long. I explained to her all that had transpired between you and I. She forgave me my trespasses and invited me to a bar-b-que the Drama Department was hosting behind the main theatre on campus. It would be on Sunday. All day. She felt I needed to socialize. I accepted.

Sue brought Maul to the affair. Jay, Dina, Clark, Connie
Steven, the entire gang was all in attendance. Jay wanted to
fuck me on the catwalk. I declined his offer, stating that I
no longer had an interest in sex.

Maul lunged at me and swiped my hot dog. Sue leashed
her and threatened to take her home. I didn't want that.

"She's fine," I said.

"She knows better," said Sue.

"We all know better, but we continue to do as we wish."

"I know, but she's here to set an example for the rest of
us."

Maul nestled next to me, as if hiding from her mother.
"See?" I said. "She knows she screwed up. She's sorry." I
bent over to give her a hug. A wet nose and sloppy tongue
washed over my face. That devilish spark was back in her
eye. Sue finally smiled.

"I heard about Rex," she said.

"Well," I shrugged. "I can't make him what he's not."

"You're lucky," she said. "I never get excited over
anyone. I'll probably die a spinster."

"I should hope that I will."

"What about Taylor?"

"What about him?"

"He's still working over at the restaurant. You should
stop by and see him."

"I don't think so," I said. "He's off on his own course
now."

"He's not seeing anyone," she said. I shot her a curious
glare. "We talk now and then," she admitted. "He's still
hung up on you."

"Rex talked to him. Did you know that?" Sue grew
crimson.

"You did!"

"Taylor mentioned it to me once."

"What else do you know?"

"Not much, honestly. He was very jealous of Rex."

"Well, that's all done and gone," I said.

"You're taking it well. A year ago we would've been

scraping your drunken ass up off the ground by this time."

"I guess change is inevitable."

Maul strained at her leash, fuelled on by the scent of grilling meat. I let Sue go, then walked back through the loading dock doors and out onto the main stage of the theatre. I loved that large black space. It was an illusionist's world. Any imagined scene could have license to live in that space. I imagined my own scenes - of you, tired of peace, abandoning that woman and returning to me. That battle wasn't over for me. Not by a long shot. You had always come back before. You would do so again. There was a course in miracles and I'd signed up for the first class.

Jay and Clark intercepted me as I made my way to the restroom. Much of the old gang was together. They all wanted to strike out for the Odessy as a sort of last hurrah. I felt good, secure in my fantasy about you. I went with them.

✻ ✻ ✻ ✻ ✻

Rick wasn't working that night. Some other young man with muscles that would've made Michelangelo proud, stamped our hands at the door. The music instantly fed my good mood, making me move out with my crowd onto the almost vacant dance floor. We danced randomly within our group, encouraging strangers to join up with us and widen our circle of bodies - all dancing our way to ecstacy.

✻ ✻ ✻ ✻ ✻

I was wringing with sweat when I stepped out onto the patio to cool down. The open air gas fire burned bright, warming me a bit against the night chill. A young woman bounced up and proffered her hand.

"Hi!" she said.

"Hi," I said.

"Don't you remember me? I'm Andrea."

"Taylor's friend. Yes! How are you?" I asked. Her hair had grown out and she'd shed twenty pounds. She looked quite the picture standing there in her 1950's prom dress.

"Ex-friend," she said. "He moved out of my place eons ago."

"Oh," I said. "I haven't seen him in months, either."

"He was too weird for me. Always coming on to me, wanting to experiment with a girl or do God knows what."

Some blond queen with luxurious, feathered hair came up and whisked Andrea away. I was glad of that. Jay caught up with me, eyeing Andrea's friend as they pranced on into the club.

"He's a good fuck," Jay said.

"No doubt you'd know," I said.

"We're heading back."

"So soon?"

"I made my score. Clark's tired and the others have early classes."

Everyone met up at the front door while Dina did her usual head count. All assembled for only a second, then we went on our separate ways.

*****

I sat up front with Clark on the ride back home. Jay and his conquest were tonguing each other's brains out in the backseat. Clark turned on the radio to drown out their obnoxious sounds. His car only had AM radio, so the pickings were slim. Bad music or the news. He opted for the news - local news and traffic reports.

The announcer glossed over a traffic accident on the 405 freeway, just north of Long Beach, then went on with some nonsense about President Carter. Clark changed the station again, settling for a country and western station. He said that type of music jarred him awake.

It was a quick ride to my new apartment. Clark dropped me at curbside then blasted away. I went in and fell straightaway into bed to sleep the first truly peaceful sleep I'd had in some time.

*****

Much of that Monday morning was uneventful. Classes and breaks. Small talk and large, styrofoam cups of bad coffee. It wasn't until one-thirty that afternoon that everything toppled. I had just come out from my stagecraft

125

class when I spotted Taylor sitting on the edge of a large concrete planter just outside the building. I was more than surprised to see him there, chewing nervously on his nails. Something wasn't right with him. He looked up at me with hollow eyes.

"I'm sorry," he said.

I didn't want to become annoyed with him. I knew that would mean that we'd have another argument. I sat down next to him as my classmates wandered off. "Sorry about what?" I asked as I took his hand from his mouth.

He pulled back a bit, as if shocked. "You don't know?" he said.

"Did Fahad come back?"

"No!" he said. "About Rex!"

"What? He's still talking to you about me?"

Taylor flushed white. "He's dead." A brief moment, then my anger took hold of my hand and I slapped him. He didn't flinch. "It's true," he said.

I hoisted up my backpack and walked on. Taylor caught up to me and yanked me around. There was desperation in that grip of his. I stared him down.

"What the fuck do you want from me, Taylor?"

"Last night. He and two other cars were in a pile up on the San Diego freeway."

"This isn't funny."

Taylor exploded. "It isn't fucking funny!" he shrieked. "He's dead! He was coming down to meet me at a bar in Long Beach!"

I remained stoic. Taylor shot up his hands in a shrug of disgust and backed away. I said nothing. Could say nothing. He didn't leave. His body quaked. Tremors of emotions being stuffed back down. He leaned against a tree.

"Taylor . . ." I whispered.

"I thought he'd stood me up, ya know? So I called his work today to give him a piece of my mind. His parents, they'd told his boss what happened."

"He went to meet you," I said.

Taylor whipped around, the dragon on the attack. "Yes! He wanted to meet with me to fucking discuss you, you jackass!"

I shook my head. "They lied. His parents lied for him. He didn't like that job . . ."

"You goddamned, brick headed idiot!" he screamed. "St. Paul's Memorial Chapel in Norwalk! They've got his goddamned body! Call them!"

I took a strained breath, nodded to him, then walked on. I didn't need that kind of crap from him, I thought. Not from anyone.

My mind jelled the rest of the day. My body went through its motions detached from its spirit. It could all wait.

✳ ✳ ✳ ✳ ✳

I did call St. Paul's in Norwalk. Yes, he was very much dead. Services and burial were scheduled for Wednesday morning. The funeral director was oh so properly sorrowful in his dialogue with me. I hung up on him. My guts felt as if they'd been wrenched out of me with a rusty hacksaw. Never before had I experienced such a completely incapacitating pain. God knows how long I sobbed. Hours upon hours until the exhaustion knocked me out.

I awoke in the morning feeling as if the weight of the world's newly dead was burying me. I couldn't move, couldn't speak, could barely breathe. My bowels and bladder locked up for the duration of my stay on that bed.

It was Carl who once again came to my aid. He broke into my apartment and pulled me from my box-spring coffin. He walked me. He fed me. Talked to me until I could finally talk back.

"Why're you here?"

"Taylor called Lisa. Lisa called me," he said.

I didn't understand. I didn't want to understand. "I want to stop," I said.

"You can't hope to will yourself to death," Carl said as he held onto me. "You don't really want to do that."

"He kicked in my wall," I said as my mind tried to will my bricklayer to return to work making me strong again.

"Maybe the wall's down for good now."

"I don't want it down!" I yelled as I tried to pull away.

He wouldn't release me.

"There is no real death," he said.

"Why did you come?!"

"Because," he said softly. "Because what love he had for you isn't to be wasted. Not like this."

"This? There's nothing tangible about it now."

"Your wall isn't tangible, either."

"I need it!"

"You have a need, all right," he said. "As I have a need. I need to be here, to help you hang on to the change you were making."

I pulled away. "What change? What fucking change is that? Seems to me, I'm forever conjuring up double negatives."

"You found that you were capable of loving him and allowing him to love you."

"Yeah? Well, big fucking shitty deal."

"Fine," Carl said. "Close up. Wall yourself in. Deny him the love that did exist. Cheat him out of that now."

I slumped back down on my bed. "I feel like a jackal, separated from the pack," I said. "It's dark all around. I can't scent my way back home in the dark. There's no sight, no smell, no nothing in a void. Just blackness that just exists."

"Everything has its opposite. You have blackness within you. A blackness that seeks out decay. You also have light in you. The light that attracted him to you. You should be thankful that he wasn't so blind."

"Then why the fuck did he leave?"

"Did you take the time to see his own blackness? Did you walk in his troubling void to help him find a way out?" he asked. I didn't answer. "You both were learning, my friend. Learning about your own egos and your own selflessness. Give him that. Give yourself that much. Grant him your grace. Give him your love even now and let go of your own selfish anger and guilt. Don't be angry with anyone, for everyone was learning. Is learning."

"I love him," I said.

"I know," he said. "Would you come with me tonight?"

128

"Where?"

"Just come."

✳ ✳ ✳ ✳ ✳

We drove for about forty minutes along the freeway. When we exited and headed into Norwalk, I felt my stomach churn.

We came to a quiet cemetery. Carl led me through a maze of headstones to a fresh, unmarked grave. I sank to my knees.

"He's here with us," Carl said as he looked up into the night sky. "Allow him in. Allow him to share with you once more the love he feels."

I stretched out on the ground, next to the settling mound of soil and closed my eyes. That apple scent. Your scent. I could smell you in the blackness - smell you one last time.

✳ ✳ ✳ ✳ ✳

I never did go back to your grave. That night, when I smelled your scent in the void, as I had smelled your scent upon our first meeting, I knew you were still there for me, loving me as no one else has since. Time moved on. My abusive, vicious nature eroded as your corpse gave way to earth and your spirit soared high into the heavens. I still get misty eyed now and then when I think of the joy that you gave me.

My bricklayer's gone now. The old gang has disbanded. We all unlocked our bonds to each other, each one ascending or descending according to his or her own growth.

Time moves on even now, yet I'm still moved to smile whenever I happen upon an ancient apple tree still blooming.

129

Also Available

Packing It In
David Rees

This collection of essays, written and arranged to form a year long diary, opens with an all too brief visit to Australia, continues with a tour of New Zealand and a final visit to a much loved San Francisco, before returning to familiar Europe (Barcelona, Belgium Rome) and new perspectives on the recently liberated Eastern Bloc countries (highly individual observations of Moscow, St Petersburg, Odessa and Kiev). Written from the distinctive and idiosyncratic point of view of a singular gay man, this is a book filled with acute and sometimes acerbic views, written with a style that is at once easily conversational and utterly compelling.

'Rees achieves what should be the first aim of any travel writer, to make you regret you haven't seen what he has seen . . .'
Gay Times

ISBN 1-873741-07-3
£6.99

Vale of Tears: A problem shared
Peter Burton & Richard Smith

Culled from ten years of *Gay Times's* popular Vale of Tears problem page, this book, arranged problem-by-problem in an alphabetical sequence, is written in question and answer format and covers a wide range of subjects.

Problems with a lover? Who does the dishes? Interested in infantilism? Why is his sex drive lower than yours? Aids fears? Meeting the family? How to survive Christmas? Suffering from body odours? Piles? Crabs? Penis too small? Foreskin too tight? Trying to get rid of a lover?

Vale of Tears has some of the answers – and many more. Although highly entertaining and sometimes downright humorous, this compilation is very much a practical handbook which should find a place on the shelves of all gay men.

'An indispensable guide to life's problems big or small . . .'
                                                            Capital Gay

ISBN 1-873741-05-7
£6.99

Heroes Are Hard to Find
Sebastian Beaumont

A compelling, sometimes comic, sometimes almost unbearably moving novel about sexual infatuation, infidelity and deceit. It is also about disability, death and the joy of living.

'Highly recommended. . .'   *Brighton Evening Argus*

'I cheered, felt proud and cried aloud (yes, real tears not stifled sobs) as the plot and the people became real to me . . .'
All Points North

ISBN 1-873741-08-1
£7.50

A Cat in the Tulips
David Evans

Both in the later flush of life, Ned Cresswell and Norman
Rhodes, room-mates of pensionable age, set off on their
annual weekend visit to enjoy a traditional spring break in
a quiet Sussex village. Where angels would fear to tread, in
rushes the feisty Ned – whilst the conciliatory Norman
becomes more reluctantly involved. The village begins to
hum, including various brushes with the law, an exciting
cliff rescue, a hard-fought game of Scrabble, Agatha
Christie in Eastbourne and a dreaded Sunday sherry party,
the weekend lurches socially from near disaster to
neocataclysm. Further complications ensue, despite Ned's
forceful objections, when the currently catless Norman falls
in love with an irresistible pussy looking for a new home.
Comedy and thrills combine in this delightful and most
British of novels.

'It's like Ovaltine with gin in it.'
               Tony Warren, creator or Coronation Street

ISBN 1-873741-10-3
£7.50

Summer Set
David Evans

When pop singer Ludo Morgan's elderly bulldog pursues
animal portraitist Victor Burke – wearing womens'
underwear beneath his leathers – to late night Hampstead
Heath a whole sequence of events is set in train. Rescued
by the scantily clad and utterly delicious Nick Longingly,
only son of his closest friend Kitty Llewellyn, Victor finds
himself caught up in a web of emotional and physical
intrigue which can only be resolved when the entire cast of
this immensely diverting novel abandon London and head
off for a weekend in Somerset.

*'Quite simply the most delightful and appealing English gay
work of fiction I've read all year. . .'*   Scene Out
'A richly comic debut. . .'   Capital Gay
'Immensely entertaining. . .'   Patrick Gale, Gay Times

ISBN 1-873741-02-2
£7.50

Unreal City
Neil Powell

One week in a hot August, towards the end of the twentieth century, the lives of four men overlap and entangle, leaving three of them permanently uprooted and changed. *Unreal City* is their story, told at different times and from their various points of view. Set partly in a London nourished by its cultural past but oppressed by its political present, and partly in coastal East Anglia, it is also the story of two older men – an elderly, long silent novelist and his retired publisher – whose past friendship and subsequent bitterness cast unexpected shadows over the four main characters. *Unreal City* is about love and loyalty, paranoia and violence, the tension of urban gay life in the century's last decade but it is about much else too: the death of cities; the pubs of Suffolk; the streets of London, and the Underground – in more than one sense; Shakespeare's *Troilus and Cressida*; the consolation of music; the colour of tomatoes, and the North Sea. It is a richly allusive, intricately patterned, and at times very funny novel.

'*Unreal City* is brilliant, understated, but powerful and should
have a wide-appeal '   *Time Out*
'*Excellent. I suggest you buy it immediately.*'   *Gay Times*
'*An excellent, extremely satisfying novel.*'   *The Pink Paper*

ISBN 1-873741-04-9
£6.99

Ravens Brood
E F Benson

The latest in our highly successful series of reprints of novels by E F Benson dates from 1934 and was almost the last novel he wrote. After *Ravens Brood*, he published only two more novels, *Lucia's Progress* (1935) and *Trouble for Lucia* (1939). By 1940, this most quintessential of Edwardian writers was dead, leaving a legacy of at least one hundred books – destined for seeming oblivion. The 'rediscovery' in the 1960s of the 'Mapp and Lucia' novels was the slow beginning of a revival of interest in Benson's work – which has subsequently produced biographies and family studies and two societies dedicated to his memory.

But *Ravens Brood* is quite unique in the Benson canon, a novel utterly unlike anything he had written before or would ever write again. 'It bristles with sexuality from the moment we meet John Pentreath, farmer and religious bigot, at his Cornish farm near Penzance,' Geoffrey Palmer and Noel Lloyd wrote in their invaluable *E F Benson: As He Was*. 'In the first thirty pages there are references to fertility rituals phallic symbols, lustful boilings in the blood, trollops, shrews, whores and harlots, a cockney strumpet, witchcraft, lascivious leers, a menopausal false pregnancy, and all seasoned with a touch of blasphemy.' The book includes, too, the character of Willie Polhaven (the name is ripe with innuendo) – perhaps the most overtly homosexual of Benson's gallery of ambiguous young men. *Ravens Brood* is atmospheric and outrageous: a rollicking good read.

ISBN 1-873741-09-X
£7.50

Millivres Books can be ordered from any bookshop in the UK and from specialist bookshops overseas. If you prefer to order by mail, please send the full retail price and 80p (UK) or £2 (overseas) per title for postage and packing to:

Dept MBKS
Millivres Floor
Ground Floor
Worldwide House
116-134 Bayham Street
London NW1 0BA

A comprehensive catalogue is available on request.